Young V

what's the story?

EASTERN COUNTIES

Edited by Steve Twelvetree

First published in Great Britain in 2003 by
YOUNG WRITERS
Remus House,
Coltsfoot Drive,
Peterborough, PE2 9JX
Telephone (01733) 890066

All Rights Reserved

Copyright Contributors 2003

SB ISBN 1 84460 274 5

FOREWORD

This year, Young Writers proudly presents a showcase of the best short stories and creative writing from today's up-and-coming writers.

We set the challenge of writing for one of our four themes - 'General Short Stories', 'Ghost Stories', 'Tales With A Twist' and 'A Day In The Life Of . . .'. The effort and imagination expressed by each individual writer was more than impressive and made selecting entries an enjoyable, yet demanding, task.

What's The Story? Eastern Counties is a collection that we feel you are sure to enjoy - featuring the very best young authors of the future. Their hard work and enthusiasm clearly shines within these pages, highlighting the achievement each story represents.

We hope you are as pleased with the final selection as we are and that you will continue to enjoy this special collection for many years to come.

CONTENTS

Brington CP School, Northampton
Lucy Henderson	1
Ella Risbridger	2

Exeter Junior School, Corby
Aiden Patrick	3
Victor Ritchie	4
Kimberley Black	5
Justine Wilson	6
Ben Young	7
Freesia-Rayne Rosser	8
Maria Harrison	9
Ross Hay	10
Raymond McMillan	11
Natalie Murphy	12
Cody McGhee	13
Liam Bradley	14
Barry Purdom	15
Marko Vucenovic	16
Adele Hutchison	17
Kieran McKenna	18

Heatherton House School, Amersham
Alexandra Bentley	19
Francesca Weil	20
Fiona Rackley	21
Emma Riley	22
Vivien Hinds	23
Claire Richardson	24
Ciara Halpin	25
Ellie Haggart	26
Lydie Harrison	27
Hannah Wills	28
Emma Walker	29
Marlene Lees	30
Alice Court	31

Chloe Townsend	32
Anya Ratnavel	33
Bliss Jennings	34
Philippa Johnson	35
Jessica Moore	36
Verity Heath	37
Deborah Cross	38
Jessica Valdez	39
Danielle Hollander	40
Katherine Parkinson	41
Hannah Eckersley	42
Nathalie Harasyn	43
Sarah Newberry	44
Jessica Gibson	45
Kate Sophoclides	46
Lauren Mawdsley	47
Katie Miller	48
Rakhee Patel	49
Katie Fenton	50

Kings Hedges Primary School, Cambridge

Sophie Moseley	51
Jemma Dean	52
Zoe Wisbey	53
Rebecca Hunneyball	54
Chelsea Hider	55
Kizzy Creasey-Keeler	56
Ashraf Ali	57
Ryan Collins	58
Alice Tansley-Binderman	59
Charlotte Andrasi	60
Madeleine Crofts	61
Nicola Bailey	62
Jamie-Lee Anderson	63
Kyle Lavender	64
Adam Mayes	65
Gabriel Silva	66
Zoe Mackey	67

Maidwell Hall School, Northampton
- Charlie Bailey — 68
- Robert Newton — 69
- Henry Ferrari — 70
- Matthew Wiley — 71
- Sebastian Tiley — 72

Middleton Primary School, Peterborough
- Rebekah Saunders — 73
- Jonathan Feltell — 74
- Matthew Fynn — 75
- Yvonne Jones — 76
- William Lobley — 77
- Grace Summon — 78
- Amy O'Malley — 79
- Abigail Sykes — 80
- Danny Mills & Ryan Manning — 81
- Chantelle Cox — 82
- Maxine Taylor — 83
- Emma Cattermoul — 84
- April Cole — 85
- Adam Burnham — 86
- Ryan Howden — 87
- Daniel Bailey — 88
- Hannah Stannard — 89

OrtonWistow Primary School, Peterborough
- Chris Porter — 90
- Grace Mills — 91
- Sarah Arthur — 92
- Natalie Mackle — 93
- Craig Chalmers — 94
- Helen Walden — 95
- Antonia Collison — 96
- Lee Bearley — 97
- Sean Watson — 98
- Robert Doyle — 99
- Michael Wright — 100

Natalie Edwards	101
Matthew McKee	102
Verinder Sander	103
Alex Wilde	104
Ross Weatherburn	105
Alice Chegwidden	106
Elliot Rippon	107
Emma Taylor	108
Bethany Becconsall	109
Rachel Freemantle	110
Ellis Bunn	111
Jake Gauder	112
Lewis Brookbanks	113
Jasmine Ling	114
Jemma Keulen	115
Ben Brown	116
Krissie Dickens	117
James Harper	118

St Mary Magdalene RC Combined School, Milton Keynes

Owen Jones	119
Rachael Cunliffe	120
Alyssa Ash	121
Tanya Frayne	122
Abigayle McCue	123
Nicki O'Hagan	124
Claire Ennis	125
Kodjo Okutu	126
Adam Danielewicz	127
Antony Bailes	128
Kelly-Ann Smith	129
Natasha Evans	130
Ramy Saad	131
Emlyn Northcote-Rojas	132
Abby Linehan	133
Alison Carter	134
Angela Mulé	135
Emily Farrier	136

Sarah McGlynn	137
Nicole Hawes	138

Thomas Eaton Primary Schoool, Wimblington

Jade Kavaliauskas	139

William Austin Junior School, Luton

Tahmina Begum	140
Marcus Doyle	141
Aksa Ahmed	142
Chloe Organ	143
Alice Trotter	144

Woodnewton Junior School, Corby

Siân McIsaac	145
Savannah Cook	146
Zoë Johnson	147
Sophie McShane	148
Shannen Garfitt	149
Opal Gilchrist	150
Callum Raine	151
Curtis Dennison	152
James Beattie	153
Andrew Payne	154
Mark Taylor	155
Daniel Murray	156
Alice Dunn	157
Clark Usher	158
Ryan McKimm	159
Liam Jackson	160
Tayla Marshall	161
Llwyd Campbell	162
Rachael McAllister	163
Hayley Skinner	164
Jack Barwell	165
Siân Davis	166
Rebecca Curtin	167
Melissa Vaghela	168

Dalian McGuffie	169
Kelsey Raffo	170
Jennifer Morgan	171
Ryan Britton	172
Luke Slater	173
Brandon Midlane	174
Nicola Gemmell	175
Hayley Gray	176
Jack Sheridan	177
Lauren Honeyman	178
Catherine Creedon	179
Cerys Russell	180
Jessica Bellew	182
Kaisie Flanagan	184
Rebecka Heath	185
Demi Weston	186
Melissa Ward	187
Ricky Murray	188
Deanna Barley	189
Kate Inglis	190
Demi Garvey	191
Demi Johnson	192
Courtney Crawford	193
Emily Tierney	194
Kimberley Briglin	195
Ciara Haughey	196
Jake Martin	197
Sarah Russell	198
Jessica Coull	199
Charlotte Roberts	200
Nicola Miller	201

The Stories

DANCE

'Well done Annabel!' Miss Bell said as she smiled.
Annabel blushed, her cheeks turned rose-pink.

Annabel Slinn was a 17-year-old ballerina. She was brilliant at dancing, in fact she was better than her teacher was. She danced with a boy called William. They had already won three golden awards, seven silvers and one bronze. All this went downhill when . . .

'Have a nice weekend,' William called.
'I will,' she answered as she started to walk backwards into the road.
'Watch out!' William yelled.
It was too late. Annabel screamed as the lorry hurtled towards her. It hit her. Annabel fell to the ground. That was when her talent went down the drain.

That night she was taken to hospital. When she got out, the first person she saw was William.

During the next few days William held auditions for his new dance partner. While he was doing this Annabel had been learning to walk again.
'Annabel,' William called.
'Yes,' she answered.
'I've got you a present, I hope you like it,' he replied as he handed her a purple box.
'You shouldn't have,' she said as she lifted the lid. Annabel gasped as she lifted out a brand new pair of ballet shoes. Annabel put them on and they fitted perfectly. William turned on the CD player and held out his hand. Annabel took it and that night they danced for two hours or more. The audience went wild, they were clapping and whistling . . .

She was cured.

Lucy Henderson (10)
Brington CP School, Northampton

COPING

The teachers at my last school said I was dumb. They didn't say that to my face, of course, but they kept looking at me with *that* look. No teachers here have called me thick *(yet)*. Ms Dowsing, my new teacher said something though. She said I was dyslexic.

Everyone always wears their thoughts on their 'sleeve', don't they? But not me. My thoughts are mine, hidden away in my own private cupboard, like the one the secretary has in her office. Especially one . . . no. I won't think about . . . Mum dying.

Dad doesn't like me talking about it. Or thinking about it. Actually, I think he'd rather I didn't think at all. You see, I'm a thinker, like Mum.

I wonder what Mum was like as a kid? I'd ask Gran, but she hates it when I mention Mum. I dunno if it'll work, but maybe if I knew about Mum, it'd help me sort out the muddle of letters and ideas in my head.
I've looked everywhere. There's only one place left. The attic. The box I'm not supposed to look in.

Wow! Mum's stuff *was* in the box - a diary, toys and photos. It's quiet here, all on my own. Suddenly, I know I'm not alone. I look over and see Dad.
'Come on, Melanie,' he says softly.
In an instant I know it'll be alright; I can see through the muddle; Mum'll be there, she's always been there.

Ella Risbridger (11)
Brington CP School, Northampton

THE HAUNTED MUSEUM

Tom was visiting the museum with his school. Towards the end of the day he decided to explore the ancient China exhibition. When he went to open the door he heard something, but paid no attention to it, so he went in anyway. Once he got in, the first things he noticed were some straw houses that looked almost real.
'Wow, they look almost real!' Tom said to himself. Then he saw a black whoosh in front of him and then he heard a panicked voice say:
'Please no, don't ki . . . *argh!*'
Then Tom's heart started to pound, then his head started to sweat and his throat dried up.
A ghostly voice said, *'Tooom cooome heeere!'*
Tom went to the voice . . . and saw a big black demon with blood on its claws and a dead body with no head in front of it.

Tom ran into one of the little houses. The scared young boy fell asleep for about five minutes and then Tom could feel something on his chest.
'*Argh!*' Tom screamed.
The demon had its claws on Tom's chest but kindly took them off before he killed him. Luckily Tom jolted fast out of the small hut, so Tom ran through the street and bumped into his teacher.

Aiden Patrick (11)
Exeter Junior School, Corby

THE HAUNTED INN

James opened his case to unpack and looked around the room. 'Hey John this room looks like that report we did for Mr Smith,' said James. There were paintings on the wall of men with old-fashioned hats on and an old wooden bed that looked like it was ready to break. Then the two boys heard a *tap, tap, tap* on the window. It had started to rain.

'They don't have a TV,' shouted John.
Suddenly they heard a *click*. They both whirled around just in time to see one of the paintings drop to the floor with a *bang*. James picked it up to hand it back on the wall but the painting floated from his hand, the window opened itself and the frightened boys heard the glass crack as the painting hit the pavement.

Later the two boys were listening to music when they heard a voice. 'Hee, hee, hee, hee. hee,' cackled the voice from nowhere.
The boys were stone stiff as a note floated to the floor. James picked it up and read out loud, 'This is my room! Get out now or you will pay!'

Knock, knock. The door opened and James' mum said, 'Your dinner is ready.'

Victor Ritchie (11)
Exeter Junior School, Corby

TOM'S MUSEUM EXPERIENCE

Tom was visiting a museum. He arrived at 12.00pm. He was looking at the pottery when suddenly he heard a *bang!* He shuddered, the bang came from a cupboard across the room. He walked over to the cupboard. Tom heard someone. It sounded like they were fighting.

Tom opened the cupboard. Someone was fighting. He said, 'Excuse me,' but the people just ignored him. He looked right into the cupboard, there was a lever. Tom pulled the lever and a secret passage opened. Tom climbed into the cupboard and went down the passage. It was slippery. Tom fell down. Someone came to him and whispered, 'Are you alright?'

He started to reply when he found himself transferred back into the pottery room. He went home but he never forgot his adventure.

Kimberley Black (11)
Exeter Junior School, Corby

THE MARWELL MURDER

For many years Lady Anne has been dead. We found some bits that she loved very well. We found her diary. One page said she had done so much work on the house, that was the 11th July. 12th July said her husband was not very happy with her.

On the 13th July Lady Anne was found dead. In her will she left: jewellery, the house and lots of money for a relative if he was still alive.

The servant lived there on her own for weeks or more. She heard the noise of jewellery and the cat. Also someone was out there looking at the garden. Lady Ann said that she would want to be buried there in the church.

People think that it is her and she is now a ghost. If you believe in ghosts go on down to explore. If you log onto www.marwell.co.uk to stay for a night or two to see if you can see the ghost.

Justine Wilson (11)
Exeter Junior School, Corby

THE HAUNTED INN

He flung his suitcase onto the floor. The room was old, the walls had gothic patterns on them. James' mother and father had gone downstairs for dinner and James said he would unpack, so he picked up the suitcase and put it on the bed. He had started. When he went to put the clothes in the drawers there was a picture on the wall. The two men in the picture looked like they had just won the lottery, but he paid no attention to it.

After he had finished unpacking he looked at the picture again. However, when he did this one of the men had disappeared and the other man's expression had changed. The confused boy thought he was imagining it so he started to potter round the room.

James had calmed down a bit until there was a smash in the other room. James ran as fast as he could but when he got there it was a broken vase. He looked around, the door handle turned, the door swung open and there was his father calling him for dinner!

Ben Young (11)
Exeter Junior School, Corby

THE HAUNTED INN

'Hello, hello, hello!' Tom's voice echoed constantly as he entered the room. It was silent. Nothing to be heard but the howling of the wind in the darkness of the night. The family had been travelling for hours and Tom decided to go off to bed.

In the night the boy woke up as he heard what sounded like coins jingling onto the table. Tom gradually turned his head left, hoping not to see an old-fashioned coin holder on his bedside, which he did see. 'You weren't there before were you?' the child asked stupidly, not knowing that he wouldn't get an answer.

'Tom, we're going out now!' called his mum.

While they were out his dad bought a paper and on the front cover it read: *Highwayman is said to haunt room 13.*

Freesia-Rayne Rosser (10)
Exeter Junior School, Corby

HOUSE ON HAUNTED HILL

The Marwell Manor is an extremely big mansion which has strange goings on. A few years ago there was a break in at Marwell Manor house and Lady Anne got murdered. People say they heard gunshots. We have not heard anything else until now.

This article is about the strange goings on at the strange and very, very, very scary mansion. There has been strange and unorthodox sounds like cats miaowing. The servant, Miss Linzianne Carison, phoned Sherlock Holmes to investigate. That's all we've heard so far.

Maria Harrison (11)
Exeter Junior School, Corby

The Haunted Inn

Tom was unpacking his bags and his best friend Tim was fast asleep snoring. Nothing could wake him up when he was asleep. The shattered boy started to put his clothes in the wardrobe, Tim started moving and speaking in his deep sleep.

A gust of grey, humid wind came in through the window, so he closed it, sat down and it happened again, but this time it was a whirl of grey, humid wind.

He had some postcards to write to his gran and grandad so he started to write. Something took over his hand, it said, 'Get out!' then it said, 'Get your friend off my bed.'

He heard money drop on the floor. Tom turned round quickly, nearly stumbling over. Tim's pillow started to move. Tim pulled it back. Everything was in the air.
'Please stop everything.'

Tom threw Tim off the bed then everything just stopped.
Tim sighed, 'What happened?'

Ross Hay (11)
Exeter Junior School, Corby

TOM'S MUSEUM EXPERIENCE

Tom was wandering around in the museum when he came to the World Wars' room. He thought about leaving and going back to the group but, 'Sothe juniors is too boring,' he said to himself. He pushed the door and it made a really squeaky creaking sound. Tom walked in and experienced a man with a moustache wearing a green suit. Therefore Tom got a little freaked.

Then he had a look around the room. Everything was grey and dull. The man in a green suit walked towards Tom. Tom flinched and the man walked right past him. Tom whispered, 'Hello.'
No reply.
Tom asked, 'Excuse me who are you?'
There was still no reply.
The man left the room, then came back five minutes later with some matches and walked right past Tom again and went over to a blanket. He pulled it off. It was a *cannon!* He lit the wire and bellowed, 'Ready aim!'
Tom tried to run but the door was locked, the cannon was coming at him then everything faded away. Tom ran back to the group, but nothing would make sense to Tom.

Raymond McMillan (10)
Exeter Junior School, Corby

SOMETHING GHOSTLY GOING ON

In this lovely countryside stands Marwell Manor, a lovely mansion that everyone enjoys looking at. In this mansion lives a servant but before lived Lady Anne.

Lady Anne owned this beautiful countryside house until she was murdered on the 13th July 1989 and now a servant lives there. Since Lady Anne died the lonely servant believes that there has been ghostly goings on.

This is what she says, 'I have been hearing weird things like playing with jewellery, cats and footsteps.'

We asked the public who they think could be haunting Marwell Manor. We asked the servant first. She said, 'I think it could be Lord Marwell, Lady Anne's husband coming to see his orchids.'

Then we asked J Ashton who witnessed the will. She thinks it's Lady Anne because she wanted to live there all her life and be buried there.

So do you believe in this story? If so it's on television 17th July 1991 or www.marwellmanor.com.

Natalie Murphy (11)
Exeter Junior School, Corby

Haunted Inn

Donna jumped into her bed that was as thin as a coffin and lay there trying to avoid her school friends in the opposite room.

It was morning now. Donna sat up and looked around her small room. It looked old with dark red walls with cobwebs in every corner. 'I don't like this room,' Donna complained. The freaked out girl started unpacking, folding her clothes in a rusty metal drawer.

Knock knock. Donna rushed to the door. Finally her dinner was there but as she was eating she heard the door rattle like someone was coming in. *It's probably my teacher playing a joke,* she thought as she moved towards the door.

Suddenly there was a creak. Donna ran around the room.
'Come on Harry,' someone spoke.
'Who's Harry? Who said that?' Donna said. She knew this wasn't a joke. Donna could hear the rain hitting her window like bullets and her wardrobe slammed like thunder.
There were two men on her bed. 'Tomorrow we're robbing Battle Road,' a man spoke with a posh cockney accent. He had curly hair, a patch on his left eye. He walked towards Donna. He polished his gun. Donna couldn't swallow, her heart raced and then . . .

Cody McGhee (10)
Exeter Junior School, Corby

THE HAUNTED INN

James was unpacking with his cousin Peter, they were talking about what to do over their holiday. They were told that the room was haunted, by their friends, but they did not believe them. James' Mum and Dad were across the corridor in a room like theirs.

They heard a jingling sound, 'What was that noise?' Peter asked.
'It was just my mum and dad,' replied James.

The two boys were very tired so they went to bed. Whilst in bed Peter asked, 'Do you believe in ghosts?'
'Don't be stupid!' replied James.

The next day the two boys woke up to find a note stuck to the wall which read: *You will believe in ghosts after you stay here.*

That night the windows started rattling violently, this was going on for another week and when they got home, they did believe in ghosts.

Liam Bradley (11)
Exeter Junior School, Corby

THE HAUNTED INN

James was unpacking his bags. He put all the clothes in the drawer and put his laptop on the table when he heard a loud scream, he looked out of the window and saw a crab clipped on to a girl's finger.

He started his laptop up and went downstairs for dinner. When he came back upstairs his laptop was switched off. The boy just left the laptop and watched TV.

It was the news. It said that the inn was once owned by Ahoy, a great sea pirate and he haunts room 13 every night. James was a bit spooked because he was in room 13 but he didn't believe in ghosts or any other monster, so why should he believe in Ahoy the pirate?

Then he heard a bang from the bathroom. There was a skeleton in the bath! It jumped up and grabbed James' hand - then James woke up, it was all a dream!

He heard a noise from the bathroom, like in his dream, he feared entry but he went in but it was only his dad. 'Phew!' James said, wiping his head.

All his possessions were on the floor and he found this note:

> 'I am Ahoy the ghost pirate - *get out* of my inn or suffer a life of torment.
>
> Ahoy.'

Barry Purdom (10)
Exeter Junior School, Corby

MWAHAHAHA! THE VOICE OF LADY ANN?

Strange goings on have been happening in the famous Marwell Manor, a couple of weeks ago. Marwell's countryside is famous for ghosts and ghouls and this is another to add to the collection . . . or is it?

Sounds were heard by a servant. The sounds were the rattling of jewellery, Dabbles the cat, she also sighted someone looking at the orchids, strangely. The spooked servant is shocked because the house has been empty for fourteen years. The servant told us exclusively, 'I am very shocked because I should be the only person in the manor.'

We found out that in her Will (Lady Ann's) she wanted to live there forever and even to be buried there.

The police are after: J Ashton, the servant, M E Thief and Lord Ashley. 'If you've seen these people/ghouls, please call 999,' PC Anonymous said, 'these are really dangerous people/ghouls on the loose!'
The public can view the house. For more information call 118888 or visit http://www.Marwell Manor.com or watch Holiday 2005. Friday 16th December 2003, BBC1 or Crimewatch UK, BBC1, Friday 16th December, 2003 at 9 o'clock.

Marko Vucenovic (11)
Exeter Junior School, Corby

THE HAUNTED INN

James had just arrived at the hotel but didn't want to share a room with his parents so he was moved into room number 13.

James was very pleased with the room, he was even more pleased with the picture on the wall because it reminded him of a school trip.

'Oh no, it's raining,' James said sadly. He thought that as soon as he was happy, it had to rain.

Next, he was bored. He got out his laptop and went on the Internet.
Creak! James jumped and said, 'Who's there?' No one answered, but there was a note at the bottom of the bed which said 'Get out of my room'!

James was spooked out, he ran to the door but it was locked and the key was floating around the room. 'Let me out!' James said.
'Only if you stay out of this room forever!' said a voice.
'Y-y-yes!' said James.

He grabbed the key, unlocked the door and ran down the corridor where he bumped into his dad and said, '*Now* I want to share a room with you!' And he ran into his dad's bed.

Adele Hutchison (10)
Exeter Junior School, Corby

THE HAUNTED INN

When Tom was unpacking his bags, he was sharing a room with his friend and Tom wanted to look around his room.

It smelled funny, so he opened the window and his friend heard a noise coming from the bathroom. Tom went to look, no one was there. Tom went out of the bathroom and out of the hotel. So Tom went to look around. He saw a floating bag in the air, so he went back inside the hotel and then there was a *bang!* It was the door.

Tom jumped against the wall . . . he turned round to find that there was a six foot man with no head!

Kieran McKenna (11)
Exeter Junior School, Corby

A Day In The Life Of A Car

I am a dark blue Volvo. I have been on the road for fifty years. My driver is called Ernie Been. I'm getting a bit rusty now, I'm still a taxi sort of thing.

On Friday I was taking the Ratnavel family to the cinema. Anya was eating an ice cream, it was rather annoying, it went all over my seats.

Finally we reached the cinema. They gave Ernie four pounds and said, 'Thank you!'

When we got back to the garage, Ernie gave me a good scrub. The next customer we had was at 4 o'clock that afternoon. It was Mrs Furdark and she needed a lift to the market. I drove a long way, I had to drive to London and we were in Aylesbury. It took us an hour to get to the market, then we were to pick her up again at 5.45pm. Ernie drove back to Aylesbury and at 5.45pm we went to pick up Mrs Furdark.

At 6 o'clock we had a very important person to pick up. It was the Prime Minister, Ernie was shocked. He went and washed me and made me smell nice inside. Then he oiled the rusty bits which squeaked. Ernie then put on his best suit and drove off.

We picked up the Prime Minister and he said he would like to go to Buckingham Palace. We reached Buckingham Palace just as the clock struck six. He gave Ernie twelve pounds.
'Thank you,' he said.

Ernie drove back and then it was 8 o'clock and it was time to go to bed.

Alexandra Bentley (9)
Heatherton House School, Amersham

A Day In The Life Of A Limousine

I am a limousine. I've been driving for ages. I had a terrible day last week - I'll tell you my story.

In the morning a little girl called Emily was eating some crisps and she got into the car. She was very young so she was a bit noisy. She spilled her food all over my seat. My owners had it cleaned in a flash though. I hoped the day would get better from then on.

At lunchtime, a naughty boy got in and he was the meanest in his class. I just behaved normally thinking nothing had changed. This boy looked older that the girl but behaved much worse. He jumped and he screamed as loud as can be. At last he was dropped off at school as it only takes ten minutes to get there. I was glad when that journey was over. After school he hopped back in and twisted and broke the radio. Then came the repair people.

In the afternoon a young man came to drive me to a pub where he had a date. He had only just got his licence and I was afraid that he would get me into another accident. We had almost got there when there was a loud bang. He'd bumped into a bush and went through a gate and landed in a pond. This really confused me, I felt very dizzy. I hope tomorrow is not as much trouble.

Francesca Weil (8)
Heatherton House School, Amersham

A Day In The Life Of Two Pictures

Once there were two pictures above a fireplace in a dining room. There was a boy on the left and a girl on the right.

One day Peter and Rose, who owned the house, went out for a walk. When it had gone quiet the girl and the boy got out of the pictures. They were magic pictures! The girl took her wooden skipping rope and the boy took his hoop and stick and went out of the room. First they went into the kitchen. The little girl skipped and the boy ran after his hoop.

Then they went into the sitting room.
The girl said, 'Let's turn the light on.'
So they did.
Then the boy rolled his hoop and knocked a table over and smashed a vase. They tried to put it back together again but they couldn't. Then they heard the key in the door and ran back into the dining room with their toys and jumped back into the pictures.

Rose and Peter came in and went into the sitting room and found the light on and the broken vase on the floor. Then they went into the dining room and looked at the pictures and noticed that something was wrong. They couldn't think what it was but then they realised that the boy was in the girl's picture and the girl was in the boy's picture. They looked at each other in amazement.

Fiona Rackley (9)
Heatherton House School, Amersham

A Day In The Life Of A Window

Hello, I'm a window. I live in a very old house in the city. I'm a miserable window for nobody has lived in this house for years. I cannot see the wonders of the world because, over the years, I have become dusty. The days are always dismal, I cannot see the children playing in the park merrily. Today is just as drizzly and rainy as always.

The rain is trickling down my face. There are no birds singing, I hear a creaky sound as if the door is being opened. Footsteps! I can hear something wandering around but what is it? I don't know!

The footsteps get louder and louder, heavier and heavier. Something is coming right at me. I can't stop it. The door is opening, I'm sure. There is a blur of colour right in front of me. It lifts up what looks like a pink stick attached to another multicoloured stick. At the end of the pink stick is a bottle of some sort. It squirts a liquid at me. It stings. It puts the bottle down and lifts up what looks like a cloth and wipes me clean. I can see! It's amazing!

It's a woman, a kind-looking woman. I smile at her and she smiles back. Now I can see the sky, clouds, children and all my friends, sparkling in the sunshine, polished, just like me. At last the house has a new family.

Emma Riley (9)
Heatherton House School, Amersham

A Day In The Life Of A Taxi Driver

I'm a taxi driver. I've been a taxi driver for 50 years and I'm getting a bit old now.

Being a taxi driver can be fun because you meet so many interesting people. Sometimes I meet famous people like Britney Spears and Tony Blair.

Yesterday was such a busy day, I started in London with a very grand lady passenger who wanted to go to Windsor Castle. She was dressed in a pink fluffy coat with a poodle in a pink fluffy coat, just like her owner.

The lady was wearing a pink glittery dress underneath her pink fluffy coat. When I dropped her off, she scooped up her poodle and got out and nearly tripped over.

Then I had lunch and collected another customer. He was going to work. I've met him before, his name is Bob Wright. He wanted to go to Uxbridge, so I took him. The place he works at is called F Hinds, it's a jewellery company which sells rings, bracelets, necklaces and watches.

After that I went to the taxi rank and had a chat with my friends. They told me what they all did. They always seemed to have more interesting days than I did. But I don't really care, I hope tomorrow is going to be a fun time. I hope it isn't busy!

I'm really looking forwards to the weekend because I'm going to watch the Watford v Arsenal football match. It will be fun, I'm sure.

Vivien Hinds (8)
Heatherton House School, Amersham

A Day In The Life Of A Poncuss

I expect you've never heard of me. Well you wouldn't have seeing that I lived over ten thousand years ago, but I'm a Poncuss.

I'm the front of a pony and the back of a peacock. I have pearly, cream-blue wings and a long, golden, flowing mane.

One day last winter, something terrifying happened. I woke up to the smell of strawberries and all the trees were covered in a red snow. It was midnight, as we Poncuss' wake at night.

My tummy was rumbling and my feathers were drooping so I decided to search for food. I was trotting along when I saw flames rising up in the distance. Something was wrong so I started to gallop. As I got closer I saw a fiery monster had trapped my family in his green, blue and white flames.

Where were my magical powers? Disaster! I'd forgotten them and I began to panic. I looked down at the snow. Suddenly I remembered, I fanned my beautiful, feathery, green-blue tail and spread out my wings. I flew up into the dark sky and pointed my tail towards the monster.

A snowstorm started with a whistling wind and the fiery monster began to fade away. Eventually he disappeared into the melting red snow.

My family was safe, away from danger. I could once again trot off in search of food.

Claire Richardson (9)
Heatherton House School, Amersham

A Day In The Life Of A Shoe

Hi, I'm a left shoe.

Here I am sitting in Jessica's wardrobe which is blue. I am red and blue, I'm waiting for Jessica to put me on.

'Mum, I'm putting my shoes on,'
'Don't be too long, I'll be in the car,' said Mum.
Yes, Jess is putting me on.
'Now I've got to buckle you up.' said Jess.
Here we go into the car, ha we're going fast.
'Mum, can I have a mint?' Jess said.

She's always asking for food, can't she ever stop. Yes, we're here! Oh look, a place called Pizza Hut.

'Hello, could I have a salami and pepperoni pizza and another salami pizza?' asked Mum
This is delicious.

'Time to go! Come on Jess hurry up, I'm waiting in the car!' said Mum

Oh now we're going to the cinema. I wonder what we're going to see?

'Guess what we're going to see, Jess?' said Mum.
'S Club!'
'Correct.'

Jess lifted me up, oh look there's Hannah with her blue eyes and rock 'n' roll John.

'That was great Mum!' said Jess.
'Yeah, it really was.' Mum replied, 'I'm glad you enjoyed it.'

Now it's time to go home, Jess is really tired, hopefully tomorrow won't be such a tiring day for me.

Ciara Halpin (8)
Heatherton House School, Amersham

A Day In The Life Of A Mirror

Hello, my name's Mirror, well that's what people call me. To me, my life is very boring. I bet after you hear this story, you'll think it is too. The reason for this is because all I do is watch people looking at me.

Okay, first there's Amy, a girl with the clothes that say *clash!* Here she comes now and she'd better take off those weirdo shorts with the pink top. *Yuck!* Now there's Tom, the vain freak and to prove it, right now he's saying to himself, 'You handsome, fine young man. You look great!' *Paa!* Yeah, right, what is he thinking?

Alright, now here comes the worst of all. Her name is Mrs Loat. Look at her, she's wearing a sun hat, scarf, goggles and oh my goodness, she's still in her underwear!

Finally it's past Sunday and it's Monday! The start of my holiday, because Amy and Tom are at school and Mrs Loat is at work. Oh darn! Hold on, it's Inset day, that's when children at school get a day off! I think I can hear music downstairs. Oh no wonder, it's Amy's birthday.

Here they all come, getting ready for the disco. Look at one of Amy's friends, she's wearing too much lipstick, so she looks like a tart and she's wearing too much blusher so she also looks like a China doll.

Well, that's all I've got to tell you and now you know what it's like being me.

Ellie Haggart (10)
Heatherton House School, Amersham

A DAY IN THE LIFE OF A BUSY MUM

6.00am	I had to wake my children and have a shower and make the children shower too. I then had to get the breakfast ready.
7.00am	Have breakfast then brush our teeth, get boys break and bags packed.
7.30am	I get the boys in the car and the dog in the car also and go off to school.
8.00am	Just dropped off the boys, now I'm going to take the dog for a walk.
9.00am	I took the dog home then I went shopping for food and clothes for myself. I am off to work now. I work in an office for two hours 10.00 to 12.00 I hate it when it's a hot day because it's hot and stuffy in the office.
11.00am	I am having a break now. I have black tea with biscuits.
12.00am	I went home and made lunch for myself. I had spaghetti and salad and tea.
13.00pm	Now I'm going to wash up and tidy the children's room. They have put their toys all over the house.
14.30pm	I am having a break and afterwards I have to take the cat to the vet then off to school to pick the children up.
15.15pm	The cat has a cold. I'm at school. Here come the children!
15.45pm	We're at home again and the children are doing their homework and I'm helping them.
16.00pm	I'm making dinner, it's the same as at lunchtime.
17.00pm	I'm ironing some clothes for school
18.00pm	Dinner, then brush the children's teeth, then bed.
20.00pm	Bedtime - another exhausting day!

Lydie Harrison (10)
Heatherton House School, Amersham

A DAY IN THE LIFE OF SPUNKY THE SNAIL

Hi, I'm Spunky. Spunky the snail.

Now before you say, *'Great, stupid snail story!'* I would just like to say a snail's day is very interesting. I, Spunky the snail, am a rare type of snail. A Gibberland Slimetop. But anyway . . . back to my day.

Many people may ask what a snail eats for breakfast. I, right now, am eating juicy, crunchy leaves. For lunch I think I will feast on Mrs Marigold's pansies or maybe a nibble of Mr Allotment's cabbages. See, I told you a snail's day was super-cool but food isn't the only super-cool thing in my day.

Now I have had my breakfast I am going to go to the snail gym since I am so fat. That is only because food is never scarce in the town of Growmore. Anyway, back to the gym. I'm outside the gym, I've spotted Mr Radish's plums. They're on the ground. I . . . um . . . well maybe I could take a small nibble. No one would notice. It's either gym or early lunch. Oh well, I can go to the gym after lunch. Now over to those plums. Yum!

It's teatime, what shall I have? I'm drawn between Mr Pottingshed's tomatoes and Mrs Growell's spinach. Choices, choices! I think I'll go with the tomatoes. No slug pellets to dodge! After tea I'll crawl under my stone and to go sleep. Ahhh!

Hannah Wills (10)
Heatherton House School, Amersham

A DAY IN THE LIFE OF A RABBIT

We are really early risers, Lettuce and me. We're always hungry so we run into our rabbit run and munch on all that sweet juicy grass. We do this every day, early in the morning.

I'm so excited, I'm going to school with Rebecca, I'm her favourite rabbit, she says I'm adorable. I wonder what her friends will think of me, although she talks about Alice as a mean, selfish person.

Here she comes now! Oh, she's got that horrible rabbit cage, but . . . it's got food in! I'm definitely going in there, yum - carrot, crunchy lettuce, sliced cucumber - delicious!

Into the cage, running straight to the food and well worth it too, bye everyone! I'll tell you about all of my adventures later.

That journey was uncomfortable, stop bumping me! I've just arrived at school. What's that I can hear? Screaming, laughing. There are loads of children running about, happily. Oh . . . oh dear, they're all running towards me like massive giants towering over me. They're softly stroking me, how lovely, on my back, left a bit, perfect! How soothing, gorgeous! *Ding-dong!* Oh, do you have to stop? I was really enjoying that.

Bouncy! Bouncy! Rebecca's walking again. What's this? More food, warm carrots, smooth and sweet, just how I like them. Where are you going without me? Come back! Must be those lessons she talks about.

We're on the move again. Home! I don't believe that my visit is over so soon.

Down I go back into my hutch, I am tired. Time for bed and dreaming of carrots.

Emma Walker (9)
Heatherton House School, Amersham

A Day In The Life Of A Hamster

I am in a pet shop, in a tank, bored as ever. Everything is dirty. People from the outside world look at us and say, 'Oh, how cute, can I buy him please?' Whereas I think that they are so stupid because they always pick the greedy ones. I am the only one left. Everyone walks past and says, 'No!' I sometimes wonder why?

But suddenly a man looks at me with a smile on his face and I am thinking to myself, *is this the one?* He says to the shopkeeper, 'Please can I take this hamster?' in his manly voice.

Then the shopkeeper opens the tank and picks me up and puts me into a box where everything sounds muffled. It all feels different at the moment. I can't see where I'm going but I can hear a very loud noise and I'm shaking about. It feels like a funfair ride but I'm not sure whether I like this one!

Suddenly the loud noise stops and everything goes still and quiet. I feel like I'm being carried then the box opens, it's bright and a hand takes me out.

The hand puts me in a *clean* cage, to my surprise and gives me *clean* water and *clean* food! This must be my new home now.

Marlene Lees (8)
Heatherton House School, Amersham

A Day In The Life Of A Taxi Driver

Hi, I'm a taxi driver, I'm called Tom and I'm 24 years old. Today my shift is 9.00am until 6.00pm. At 6.00pm I drive into the taxi station for another guy to drive the taxi.

So I'd better get started. I have a screen in my taxi to tell me what address I need to go to and today it says: Gooseberry Lane, 24 Avenue Road.

'Come on into the taxi!'
As the woman and her husband stepped into the taxi, they plonked a peculiar bag onto the back of my taxi seat. 'So where to?' I asked them. 'Woodnew House, 38 Middle Road,' they replied.

The next address was the Manor House but I was hungry so I stopped to get a sandwich and crisps and ate them whilst I was driving to the Manor House. When I arrived, there was a woman standing outside the house with a Tesco's uniform on. She got into the taxi and I dropped her off at the automatic doors. To my amazement, the Security of Tesco's was shouting, 'Stop that thief!' I pushed down on the accelerator as hard as I could and luckily the thief landed on the bonnet of my taxi.

In the end, the police were so pleased with me for catching the thief that they gave me an award - and that's a day in the life of a taxi driver.

Alice Court (8)
Heatherton House School, Amersham

A Day In The Life Of A Bumblebee

Hello, I am a bee and my name is Buzz. I live in a speed camera. I am called Buzz because I buzz around a lot and my mum and dad are fans of Buzz Lightyear.

Today I woke up and looked out of the window and to my surprise, I saw a car going much too fast, so I ran up a ladder and took a picture of the car. Inside the car sat an old lady with a caterpillar in her hair.

For lunch I had a honey sandwich, it was delicious, honey sandwiches are my favourite. For pudding I had honey sponge and custard, delicious!

This afternoon, my friend Ant invited me round to have a disco at his house. Ant is obviously an ant and he lives in a traffic light. When the colours on the traffic lights change, it looks like a real disco. We put the music on as well. I flew down the road for two miles until I got to the traffic lights where Ant lives. I knocked on the door and Ant opened it. I walked in and we turned the music on. We discoed for five hours and when ten o'clock arrived, I said that I had to go home. So I flew home with the flashlight I had brought with me.

At home I had my tea, brushed my teeth and watched television until my mummy said, 'Time for bed.'

I have to go now . . . *zzzzzz!*

Chloe Townsend (9)
Heatherton House School, Amersham

A Day In The Life Of A School Bag

I'm a school bag. I'm called Bad Bag and I go by my name! I am eleven years old and I am fed up with being thrown about in a box, in the playground, or dumped on the floor. I have also experienced having squashed bananas stuck to me but I always get my own back. I throw all the things in me on the floor!

Today my owner, Alex Brown, is having a school trip to Buckingham Palace to see the Queen. I decided I would call myself Good Bag. Today Alex was being a bit naughty. He pulled faces at the Queen's maids and what I found to be extremely rude, was that he threw me, spun me round and round until I was dizzy and then threw me onto the hard floor! In the end, after lunch, he had to pick me up and bring me to the Queen. I thought she looked very pretty with her diamond rings and gold earrings. As pretty as she was, she accidentally trod on me with her sharp high heels! After we saw the Queen, we went back to Alex's school, then home.

That's what it's like being a school bag. Not easy! I do hope that tomorrow will be easier and less exciting than today.

Anya Ratnavel (8)
Heatherton House School, Amersham

A Day In The Life Of A Grandfather Clock

Hello, I'm a grandfather clock and I live in the kitchen of a farmhouse in Dorset. I have stood here for fifty years and not much has changed. Every Monday Maggie comes to wind me up and she has never yet forgotten.

When I woke up this morning, it was almost breakfast time and I could hear Lucy and Ben coming downstairs. As Ben stepped into the kitchen he tripped over his Game Boy and went flying across the room.
'Ow, ow, ow! Who put that Game Boy there?' yelled Ben.
'You did, silly!' said Lucy. 'Remember? You put it there last night!'
At last Maggie came downstairs and removed the large brass key from on top of the cupboard to wind me up. After she had, she replaced the key and started to make the children's breakfast, just as I began to strike seven.

When the children were coming home from school, I struck five and when they came into the kitchen, I could see that Ben was sweaty and muddy from playing football and Lucy's hair was soaking wet from swimming. As Lucy sat down, she pulled up the typewriter and began to work on chapter five of the book she was writing. 'The Golden Horse', whilst Ben settled down to do his homework.

When everything was finished. Maggie came downstairs and said, 'It's bedtime for you two.'
So by the time I struck seven both the children were asleep. Now it's time to sleep.

Bliss Jennings (8)
Heatherton House School, Amersham

A Day In The Life Of A Lazy Lion

Rooaarr! Go away! Grr! Oh sorry, I didn't know it was you. Well, I'd better introduce myself - I am a lion.

I've just woken up (a little early actually) from a really, really good sleep. I was dreaming about chasing a zebra and then I caught it. I chewed and chewed and chewed. I was actually very glad it was very chewy because it was the most delicious piece of meat I had ever had in my life. I was just about to swallow it when I woke up. But I don't chase any zebras at all, my wife does that.

Back to the story then, I'm hungry. I think I'll go and tell my wife that she will have to go and catch some food.

When I finish eating, I always feel a bit drowsy, but today I felt particularly drowsy, which made me fall asleep right where I had eaten the zebra (this made it very difficult for the other lions to get in and have their share).

I had another really, really good dream. It was about a lion having a nap dreaming about another lion having a nap dreaming about another lion having a nap, etc!

I napped for hours and woke up just as the sun was setting, so I got up to have a walk around the Savannah before going to bed.

Philippa Johnson (9)
Heatherton House School, Amersham

A Day In The Life Of A Mirror

Hi! I'm a mirror. I live in a bathroom on a light blue wall. I arrived at this new house this morning at 4.30am. I looked at the clock on the hallway wall as I was carried upstairs. Today a man came in called Tom. He came in to have a shower and brush his teeth. Whilst he was having a shower, my face was steaming up. Aagh! I can't see.

At last the shower stopped and Tom wiped my face with a cloth. Hooray, I can see again.

Tom was brushing his teeth, he had this brown dot right at the back of his mouth. I felt like saying, *brush harder!*

Oh thank goodness, he scrubbed it out. Well, I'll see you soon.

Later on in the day a little girl came in, she must have been about twelve and very pretty. As she was looking at me, she was also saying, 'Mum, is lunch nearly ready?'
'Yes dear,' replied her mum.
So she went downstairs.

Later, after dinner, the little girl came to do her hair because it had fallen down and was messy. She looked like she had gone through a hedge backwards!

When she had eaten her dinner she went straight to bed because she was tired. She didn't have a bath or a shower. So that was my first day here with this family. And now I realise I will be hanging on this wall forever. I'm very happy, see you soon.

Jessica Moore (8)
Heatherton House School, Amersham

A Day In The Life Of A Dog

Hi, I'm Fluff, what a bad name, isn't it? Well I'm a dog. Actually the biggest miniature Schnauzer that ever lived.

My owners are called Jack and Lucy. They are twin three-year-olds and . . . ouch, Lucy's plaiting my hair. Now where was I? Oh yes, they named me.

Here's a little of my day.

I woke up this morning, well the twins woke me up. They were rocking me and my basket in the air, then dropping it. I jumped out of bed, luckily it wasn't too high.

For breakfast I had nothing. They forgot to feed me, I nearly got caught raiding the cupboard.

Later I was bundled into a car then a moment later I was led into a building with the twins. Then I realised it was 'Bring your pet to nursery' day! That was why my fur was washed and plaited. The teacher was no better than the children. 'He's bootiful!' she squealed. But after that she wasn't too sure because I tipped over jugs and chased a cat. I was sent home.

After a lunch of again zilch! I ran away. I ran for hours to a den I've been making. It's stocked with tons of food. I'm very happy here. All I have to worry about is the dog catcher. Now to plan a holiday. Probably to Hawaii. Aaah!

Thank you for listening to my day, I hope you enjoyed it. Goodbyeee.

Verity Heath (9)
Heatherton House School, Amersham

A Day In The Life Of A One-Year-Old

Everything is so big! All these things towering above my little head. I am only just as big as a cat. I don't know why I'm so little, but I know it feels strange. Look at the size of the table! Look at the size of the chair and my mum! Is everything supposed to be this big, or am I just very small?

I watch my mum move, I see how she walks on two legs. Just two. How strange, I move about on four. I can crawl very fast. I practise in the hall, I crawl to the front door and ahh! Something has got me! I wriggle, I kick and it turns me round. It's my mum!

What's she doing? She's putting me in a buggy. Yeah! We're off! Down the lane, across the road and there's the nursery! I always arrive at lunchtime. Yum!

Yawn! Food makes me sleepy. I know what I'll do, I'll go, have a nap on those bean bags. I wonder why everything is so, so . . . *zzzz!*

Ahh! What a lovely nap. Hang on, where's my mummy? Why am I still here, at the nursery? I want my mummy! But where is she? Why hasn't she come back for me? The door's opening. I hope it's my mum coming to get me, but what if it isn't? What do I do then?

Ahh! Here she is. Time to go home. Just like yesterday and the day before. I wonder what tomorrow will bring?

Deborah Cross (10)
Heatherton House School, Amersham

A Day In The Life Of A Mirror

You have no idea how many different people I see in a day. It's very interesting being a mirror but it can be quite boring sometimes. Hanging on a wall all day makes you feel numb. I've just been wiped awake by the cleaner with her disgusting-smelling spray. Time to start the day.

The first person who comes into the toilets is a man wearing baggy clothes and holding a cigarette. Oi! Can't you read, the sign says *No Smoking!* Yuk! He had just peered into me and blown a big stream of smoke into my face . . . at least there's one good smell around . . . the scent of cooked breakfast wafting in from the local café. It's a shame mirrors can't eat, that bacon smells delicious!

As the afternoon approaches, more people file in using loos and re-doing their hair. I'm getting more dirty by the minute . . . you there! Little girl! Don't turn that tap on, it . . . too late! I'm already being sprayed with soapy water. Oh no, it's the giggling girl group from yesterday. They're applying lipstick after eyeshadow in front of me. I get so bored of it. I could really do without seeing them all the time.

At last, they've gone, but leaving a mess of face powder along the sink. The smell of chips is in the air. It must be teatime. A boy's just vomited. Horrible! I'm going to go to sleep. I'm too steamed up to . . . stay . . . awake.

Jessica Valdez (10)
Heatherton House School, Amersham

A Day In The Life Of A Taxi

Yawn! I'm so tired. I was up until eleven last night and now it's seven in the morning.

I'm on my way to the Mayhews' house to pick them up and take them to Heathrow Airport. Ouch! That hurt! The Mayhews have just slammed their really heavy bag into my backside. Oh it is really killing me these days, although my owner is taking me into the garage later, which will make me feel much better.

Finally we arrived at the airport and I am now on my way to the garage for some repairs to my boot. Right, off we go!

I am driving onto this ramp and being lifted into the air. But I'm scared of heights! So I'm up here, twelve feet in the sky with all these strange men beneath me, checking for damage.

'There it is.' I hear one of them say. I am being lowered down a bit and now the cheeky devil is fiddling with my underparts!

I feel a tug. Part of me is being dragged away. Fear floods through me. Am I going to expire? Is this the end of my life? Will I be here forever? These questions are swimming around my head, when suddenly I feel a warm sensation spinning across my back and spreading around me.

The heat has gone now and I have a shiny new exhaust pipe. When I arrive home I can have a well deserved rest.

Danielle Hollander (10)
Heatherton House School, Amersham

A Day In The Life Of An Ant

Hi, I would like to introduce myself, I am King Ant. I would like to tell you about when my house roof got pulled off. I was in my house, my usual self, then suddenly I heard a clatter. *Oh,* I thought, *it must be my wife cleaning the dishes* and it was. My daughter and son were in the garden scurrying around.

Now here it comes, this is when it happened. I was just sitting there on my throne and suddenly it started to get all cold . . . and then colder . . . and colder. And then brighter . . . and brighter . . . and brighter. Then suddenly the house roof had been pulled off! All I could see was a big person rather like a giant.

My son and daughter were still outside scurrying around, I just didn't know what to do! I was just too scared to walk out incase the giant trampled on me. I just had to get my daughter and son. We were going to have to move under another plant pot. I didn't know what to do. Then the giant walked over to a different plant pot and on the way, the giant nearly stepped on my son. I screamed, 'Arrgghh!' and it made my son jump very high and land on his bottom very hard.

Katherine Parkinson (9)
Heatherton House School, Amersham

A Day In The Life Of A Newspaper

'Ouch!' I'm going through the printing process, it's like travelling on a roller coaster. My name is The Times. I'm sure my eyesight isn't working because I can see two white eyes overlooking my tummy. I seem to believe that the eyes belonged to a man with a beard, a hairy body and a pierced eyebrow. The man raised his dirty hand and a blunt pencil. 'That's good,' I chuckled quietly, he was massaging me with his pencil, now I'm worth £1.50.

Mr Lloyd from the tattoo shop rushed in and grabbed me with his big hands and raced back to the shop forgetting to pay. While he was testing his needle he read my front cover, dropping the needle on my headline. Astonished about my black printed letters spelling 'Tattoos will be banned'. 'No!' he cried, as he charged towards the door leading to the boss's office. He ripped the tattoo article out and carried on walking. The pain surrounded the letters like fur surrounding sheepskin. The tattooist knocked on the door with his fist.

As the boss opened the door sharply the man started to explain. I was then thrown into the bin.

When the dustbin men came I fell out of the bag and I was left in a murky puddle on the side of the road, I smelt of rotten eggs and cheese. That's what I call a bad day.

Hannah Eckersley (9)
Heatherton House School, Amersham

A Day In The Life Of A Pair Of Shoes

What's that noise? Why is it so dark and why am I moving about . . . ? Ouch! Someone's dropped me. Oh no! What's happening now? It's getting brighter and brighter and brighter. Ahh daylight.

I say, watch where you're putting that lace. That's my eye you're poking. People these days, I do have feelings you know. Yikes! What's that large woolly-covered thing and what is that smell? I do hope I'm not going anywhere near that!

Oh no, I'm actually attached to this smelly, woolly-shaped thing. Help! Now what's happening? I'm moving and pressure is being put on me.

Oh that's great, it's staying with me, it looks as though I have a new smelly friend. Now it looks like we're going for a walk. Oh this is disgusting. I am covered in mud. Yuck!

Ouch! Did you have to bang me against the large, black and white ball? Oh great, I've got a headache now. Oh, oh, we're on the move again. I hope I'm going back to my dark, warm home. Oww! That horrible stone scratched me. It really hurts. Oh please take me home.

At last the smelly, woolly thing has taken me off. Now I can hear a splashing sound. Argh! I'm all wet. Oh this is actually quite nice. Maybe it isn't all that bad being a shoe.

Nathalie Harasyn (10)
Heatherton House School, Amersham

A Day In The Life Of A Mirror

Hi, my name's Smear, it sounds like a bizarre name but I like it. I am a grand mirror in a ladies rest room. People look at me to see a reflection of themselves. The person who looks at me the most is Mrs Baker, who is fat and has wild ginger frizzy hair which covers her face. She always puts lipstick on and smudges it but the worst thing of all, she peers at me really closely and that's when I have to concentrate really hard especially when I think her tight dress is going to tear any moment to reveal her flabby skin. It is not a pretty sight.

There is also this girl called Kristy who is absolutely gorgeous. She wears fancy crop tops and really tight jeans. She might look nice but she is a big bully and never leaves people alone. The person who she bullies most is basically a nerd called Jenny who has curly hair and these big framed glasses.

Most of the time when Jenny is in the toilets alone she looks into me and says in the most quiet of voices, 'Whoever is listening out there, please just hear me. I wish I could look as good as Kristy. Please! Please!' Hopefully one day I could make that dream come true.

Sarah Newberry (10)
Heatherton House School, Amersham

A Day In The Life Of A Chimpanzee

Yes, I am one of those chimpanzees who everyone comes to see at the zoo. I wonder what horrible monsters are coming today? I suppose it is time to get my little chimps ready for the show.

Now, where are you? One . . . two. Oh no, where is number three? There you are, it's time for your nit picking session.

Good heavens chimpys we are on early, they've arrived. Why is it that they squash their faces against the window and make those ridiculous noises?

Come on number one, it's time for you to peel your banana, number two do your swinging act and number three well, we'll pick at your nits! And for a finale I'll scratch my bottom in public! Maybe not, here come the safari keepers. It's our turn to be released into the safari park, car trail.

This is exciting as it is my chance to get back at those funny looking squashed faces that try to mimic me through the window. Me and my chimps are being transported into the park now. Here comes some square boxes with a horn on the top, huh see how they like it when I squash my face up against their window. Then I think I'll be really cheeky and snap that thin horn on the top. I'm just not any ordinary chimpanzee, I am just as good at fooling around as you are!

Jessica Gibson (9)
Heatherton House School, Amersham

A Day In The Life Of The Queen's Daughter

Hi, I'm the queen's daughter Georgina Fox, and I'm going to tell you all about what I have to put up with.

I wake up and my mum is getting dressed in her scarlet robe and her crown. She starts singing. *Arggh!* Be quiet! The Queen is rubbish at singing, that is why she has lessons (but they don't change her voice!) The fifth headache of the week, a record.
'Come down Miss Fox,' our butler said.

Downstairs, to my surprise, I found Geoff and Steve (the interviewers). I asked Stewart to bring my breakfast up. I went to my room, the cave. My room's dark and spooky, like a bat's secret lair. I could hear Steve asking a question. But I also heard, 'Do you want to come to my party?' We talked about the party, over much deliberating, we have decided to go.

We had to dress up smartly (again) and I had to choose what she should wear. We arrived at the party and I went off whilst Mum was gurgling down wine. Mum was drunk and Steve was taking notes. I made Mum come home because I was too embarrassed there. Mum was all over the TV, I wasn't even going to go to school tomorrow because I would be teased like hell.

I walked to bed and started thinking, *what will happen when I wake up tomorrow?*

Kate Sophoclides (10)
Heatherton House School, Amersham

A Day In The Life Of An Ant

Another day of being small. Oh sorry I haven't introduced myself. I am Flick the worker ant. Well I know what you're thinking. You wouldn't want to know about a small little ant, well you're wrong! Being an ant isn't boring at all!

I am setting off to work now and I have just said goodbye to my dear family. Felicity, my wife, Fred and Frolic my two children.

It's scorching hot outside. I noticed when I was climbing out of my anthill, the temperature just hit me. Last night I went to book a hopper taxi to go to work in. A hopper taxi is just like a helicopter that takes you anywhere you like.

I arrived at HQ to speak to my boss. He is fat and greedy, just like a pig. I grabbed some lunch, a quick dandelion and buttercup sandwich. I headed upstairs, but I had to be sent back down to dig because I took too long to eat lunch! Oh dear!

I am back off home now but this time I am walking home to spend some valuable time with my family.

Lauren Mawdsley (10)
Heatherton House School, Amersham

A Day In The Life Of A Toy Dog And The Ice Cream

Hello! I would like to introduce myself. My name is . . . well I can't tell you my name because I have not been bought yet! It's really boring sitting here day after day watching people press their ugly faces on the window.

I just wish that someone would buy me, after all I am quite an attractive toy dog. I'm not really bored because yesterday I made a friend called Molly, she is a Beanie Baby.

Who's that at the door? Oh no, a little girl is coming in. What if she buys Molly? What if I never see her again? I will not have any friends!

Last night I stole an ice cream from the counter. I climbed down from my shelf, and I slipped on some wet glue and that made the Easter eggs fall down. *I would be in hot water if the owner found out*, I thought. I jumped over the crisps and onto the cold ice cream box. I opened the box and took out a Malteser because Molly said that they tasted good. Although the owner of the shop comes back at 9 o'clock, he suddenly burst through the door in rage. He picked me up by the scruff of the neck and threw me back on the shelf.

Katie Miller (10)
Heatherton House School, Amersham

THE DAY IN THE LIFE OF AN ANT

Another day of heavy footsteps slamming down on the pavement, running in and out of them as if it's a game of dodgeball, getting out of breath. Eventually find a leaf to hide under and crawl to safety. I lift over the leaf when I hear nothing and find myself in a beautiful garden. As I look up I see tall trees towering above me and a huge building which giants live in. I see a great big yellow blob shining on me and uh-oh! I hear giants smaller than the ones I see driving cars, but still huge!

Arghhh! They're trying to squish me! I'm running for my life! *Phew!* Finally they've given up. *Uh-oh!* I'm still in danger, they're getting out a huge red and blue ball. Ahead of me I see my long green food all around me and stop for a bite. Now this is really bugging me I cannot find peace anywhere I go, giants are always towering over me like a shadow! My whole life is a big game of dodgeball. At last I've been saved with a slit in the pavement. I rush towards it dodging crickets and worms.

Finally I crawl down the slit and try once again to get some peace and have a nap. But I fail again with a giant cleaning the pavement. At last the moon and stars are appearing on a black background and there are not many giants around, but there are still some animals lurking around. *Arghhh!*

Rakhee Patel (9)
Heatherton House School, Amersham

A Day In The Life Of Mr Pullitt - The Dentist

'Now, what would you like done today, Mrs Hewitt-Smythe?' I enquired, trying hard to smile.
'I would just like a 6-monthly check-up,' she replied, sounding very posh and annoyed as she had been kept waiting. Mrs Hewitt-Smythe was very rich and used to things being done her way.

She opened her mouth as wide as a lion yawning and I saw a badly crumbled tooth. I inspected it closely. 'I don't want to say this Mrs Hewitt-Smythe . . .' who looked suspiciously over her moon-shaped glasses. I took a big breath. 'You have an abscess,' I mumbled quickly. 'I will give you some antibiotics.'

11.30am - Lunch break.

12.30pm - 'Now young Master Patel there is nothing to be afraid of, you are just going to have a brace fitted,' I cooed trying to sound convincing. I put it into his mouth.
'*Aaaaggghh!*'

Mr Patel was next and he didn't cause a problem at all. He was just silent. I think it was because he had a sore throat. I put a mask on to make sure his germs didn't invade my throat!

After Mr Patel went home, I went home too, not tired, but needing to put my feet up because I had been on them the whole day. I lay back on the sofa in front of a welcoming fire . . . but then the phone rang . . . it was an emergency call out . . . but that's another day!

Katie Fenton (10)
Heatherton House School, Amersham

SECOND SPOOK

'Can you tell your sister to stop leaving muddy footprints all over the house?'

When Mum heard about this she said, 'When you hear Rachel go out, follow her.'

Rosa said, 'OK Mum.'

'Remember, try to really scare her,' reminded Mum.

That night Rosa went up onto the top of the bridge ready to scare her. A minute later Rachel went and stood under the bridge. Rosa, who was on top of the bridge, started making really spooky ghost noises. Underneath, Rachel started getting really scared.

All of a sudden, Rosa started hearing ghost noises, Rosa turned around and there she saw a ghost. 'Arrgh! a ghost!' she screamed. She staggered backwards and suddenly fell off the bridge and right onto her sister.

When she woke up the next day she was lying next to her. She whispered to Rachel, 'How are you? I didn't mean any harm.'

'I know you didn't Sis,' whispered Rachel.

Later, the doctor came and told them both they could go home.

They both said, 'We are not going home because there are ghosts!'

'There's no such thing as ghosts,' said the doctor, as he vanished through the wall.

Sophie Moseley (9)
Kings Hedges Primary School, Cambridge

A Day In The Life Of Rebecca And Jemma On Holiday

One day the sun was beaming hot. Rebecca and Jemma were going to the beach. Rebecca went for a swim and there was something underneath the water. She looked and saw it was a huge killer whale, it looked friendly, but it wasn't.

Jemma heard Rebecca shouting, 'Help!'
Jemma had realised it was Rebecca. She jumped in and got hold of one of Rebecca's legs. The killer whale was really strong. Jemma kicked the killer whale and saved Rebecca's life.

Rebecca went and sat on a chair to recover while Jemma was snorkelling in the sea. She was relaxing when all of a sudden she was underneath the water. A killer whale tipped her over, I think he wanted to play. Jemma would not play with him so he got angry and pulled her away from shore. Rebecca jumped in and got hold of Jemma's arms and brought her to shore.

Rebecca had an idea to put a netting across so killer whales couldn't get into the part near the beach. They would hurt children and adults. It was not fair when people went on holiday who wanted to have some fun. They couldn't if the killer whales came near the beach. That's why they put a netting there. They saved their own holiday and other people's by keeping the killer whales away.

Jemma Dean (10)
Kings Hedges Primary School, Cambridge

THE DEATH COACH

Every night in the abandoned church gardens there was a grim and grizzly wagon coach and horses that came. It was called by the demon of the Underworld, a ruler since she was a child of nine years old.

The deathly coach was called one silent night at the stroke of midnight, to take the victim straight to the land of fire by the black-hooded driver. But the victim indeed was the demon's own sister, so it was the demon who still cared, and sacrificed herself by taking the victim's place.

Zoe Wisbey (10)
Kings Hedges Primary School, Cambridge

EYE, EYE

'Go, go, go!' blurted Gary. 'Yes! I win and you lose, I mean maybe next time . . .'
'I'll never be any good at these new PlayStation games,' moped Robert.
'Hey, want to go to the pub?' asked Gary.
'I suppose so,' Robert grunted.
At the old pub no one was about, it was empty.
'Two lagers over here please Mike,' gleamed Gary.

At that moment a news report came on the TV . . . 'Armed madman escaped out of jail and is on the loose. There is no sign of his whereabouts and help is needed,' groaned an old news reporter's voice.
'What a load of rubbish,' tutted Gary.
'This madman also has a distinctive glass eye,' continued the reporter.
'I'm going to the loo,' sighed Gary.
There was a loud bang and some smashing noises.
'They need to get that telly fixed,' smiled Gary.

He walked back into the main part of the pub. The pub was wrecked - glasses were smashed and Mike the bartender appeared to be dead.

Robert was gone. The door was still swinging and when Gary looked in his glass a glass eye was floating in his drink. 'This can't be happening!' trembled Gary in fear.

Rebecca Hunneyball (10)
Kings Hedges Primary School, Cambridge

MATTHEW'S DREAM

Kyle was commentating Matthew while he was playing football: 'Matthew runs up skilfully with the ball. Matthew falls over and creates a handball. He's tapped the ball into the top corner! It's a goal!'

Matthew kicked the ball over the fence. Matthew was at the park.
'Unlucky Matthew, a bit more training and you will be perfect for the school team.'
'Who are you?' Matthew asked the boy.
'I'm Kyle, remember? I've just cut my hair, that's why. I'm different. I know you want to join the team. I've seen you sitting there, longing to be in the team,' Kyle said.
'No one wants me in their team, 'cause I'm useless,' Matthew moaned.
'I want you in my team. I'll have a talk with Daniel,' Kyle said.

Kyle went to talk to Daniel.
'No, no and no! He's not joining the team. He's pathetic and useless,' Daniel shouted in the training ground.
'Haven't you seen him in matches?' Kyle said.

They had a big argument and Kyle was put on the bench.
'That good-for-nothing captain! He's put me on the bench!' Kyle bellowed.
'Don't worry,' Matthew said soothingly.

The next day Kyle and Daniel argued the whole day until Kyle threatened to punch him in the head.
Daniel finally cried, 'OK, he can join!'
Daniel saw Matthew and he wasn't that bad.
'Matthew, d'you want to be captain for the next match?' Daniel asked him.
'Sure! Thanks!' Matthew exclaimed.

The next match they won, thanks to Matthew.
'I guess my dream came true!' Matthew said.

Chelsea Hider (10)
Kings Hedges Primary School, Cambridge

JELLYFISH

Mr Jelly lived in a small cottage called Oakling House. *Funny name for a cottage,* he always thought, it being a cottage, not a house.

Anyway, this story begins with Mr Jelly watching his favourite programme, when he heard a funny noise. He went outside to look.

What he found was not what he had expected, in fact, he hadn't know what to expect at all!

A small green blob type was smiling up at him. 'Hello,' it said, as Mr Jelly scooped it up. 'My ship died,' it continued.
'You can stay with me,' said Mr Jelly.

The blob turned out to be called Spike and Spike did stay with Mr Jelly but it wasn't long before he began to get homesick.

Spike gave a sigh.
'What's wrong?' asked Mr Jelly.
'I just, well . . . um.'
'You miss your home?'
'How did you know?'
'I know a lot of things. Just tell me where you live and I'll take you home tomorrow.'

Spike told Mr Jelly all about planet Jellyfish and Mr Jelly promised to take him home.

The next day Mr Jelly went to Carl's Rocket Hires and, well . . . hired a rocket. He then took Spike back to his home. Spike was very happy indeed to be with his family again and Mr Jelly will never forget him. Scout's honour!

Kizzy Creasey-Keeler (10)
Kings Hedges Primary School, Cambridge

BROKEN TRUST

'Look out!' said James. 'The crab's going to pinch you!'
'Whoops!' said David.
David had accidentally knocked over Mum's most expensive and best vase.
'Uh-oh!' said James. 'Mum's going to murder us.'
'I know,' said David, as if he was heartbroken.

'I know!' exclaimed James. 'The vase is broken into six pieces. Let's glue it together.'

After an hour they finished, but the glue wasn't dry yet.
'Kids, come on, we're going to the market stall,' shouted Mum.
'Why?' asked James.
'I'm going to sell my best vase,' said Mum happily.

This meant trouble for David and James.

When they got to the stall David and James met their arch-rival Daniel.
'Hello losers. Oh, you're selling that vase are you?' said Daniel. 'I bet it's worth more than you,' he went on.
'Oh yeah, face it, when people like you were cool, fire wasn't invented,' said James angrily.
Just at that moment, Mum picked up the vase and it broke into pieces.
'*David and James!*' Mum roared.
'Yes Mum,' said David, like an old man.
'Why did you break my vase?'
'Sorry Mum, said James.
'*Euurrhhggg!*' bellowed Mum.

The next day Mum bought a new vase which was even more valuable. David and James were playing a game when, *crash!* 'Oh no!' said James. 'Not again.'

Ashraf Ali (10)
Kings Hedges Primary School, Cambridge

A Day In The Life Of My Hamster Dee Dee

I was snoozin' happily when Count Fluffvla woke me with a long, loud, droning miaow to Ryan, who was watching the big colour box. *Surely I'm more interesting than that,* I thought. To keep fit I ran around in my little pink wheel, but unbeknown to me the cat was glaring at me.

The cat went to Ryan to get cuddled. I wanted to be cuddled, but because I bit Ryan once, they won't let me be. I needed more water, so I chewed the bars of me cage and got told of by Chris. Chris then put me on the freezer, the cold vibrating freezer. I headed the roof of my bed and I had my pee-stained cotton wool replaced with clean cotton wool.

I hid in my house, drank and ate and then I escaped by monkey-barring to the tenth part of the ten-part cage. I was out and in my toy aeroplane, when Old Fluffballs came. A single blood-red feather dangled from her regal lips. It was a gruesome sight. I flew off but she followed me everywhere, except when I swerved out of the kitchen. She slid out of the cat flap (hee-hee-hee).

Eventually I was caught and everyone went to bed. My cage door was open and my aeroplane was switched on, so I flew all over the house in darkness. The worst day turned out to be really cool.

Ryan Collins (10)
Kings Hedges Primary School, Cambridge

HEART OF DRAGON

Lisa was running out of the woods and there were wolves chasing after her. For a second she thought she saw something red, although she told herself that she didn't.

Lisa climbed up the tree. She had lost the wolves but that red thing was a dragon. It chased her. Then she dived into a meadow and she finally lost the dragon.

Next she met her friend Rosie in the meadow. She wanted to look for the dragon so they both went back to the village to get spears and bows and arrows.

They went through meadows, over hills and through valleys until they found a dark, spooky cave. They didn't really want to go into the cave.

Before they tackled the dragon they went to a village where they got food and water. In the village they met a boy called James and they told him where they were going.
'Please can I come with you?' he said.
'OK,' said Lisa.

They went to the cave and there they found a talking dragon. It was a red and yellow dragon and it said, 'Please can you take this thorn out of my wing?'
'OK,' the children said nervously and took out the thorn.
'Thank you,' said the dragon.
'I think we will just go now,' they all said together.
'I think not,' said the dragon. 'I have not eaten for years and you all look so tasty.'

Lisa threw a spear and hit the dragon's heart and it died.

The three friends went back to the village.

Alice Tansley-Binderman (10)
Kings Hedges Primary School, Cambridge

DO YOU BELIEVE IN FAIRIES

Once there was a girl called Sarah, who lived in a small, but quiet village. She had no imagination and the one thing she really did not believe in was fairies. She thought it was babyish.

When she was at school a girl called Lucy said to her, 'I've seen fairies and they write to me. Look I have a photograph to prove it.'
'Yeah, I bet you got it from the computer,' laughed Sarah. 'You're wasting my time, I have got to steal lunch money, so please move!'

Lucy never cried or anything because she knew the fairies were real. Lucy had a secret and no one knew about it. Lucy wanted to show Sarah that fairies were real so she grabbed her by the wrist.
'Get off, you big wimp,' said Sarah.
'You must come, you must!' Lucy said.

They went to the old girls' toilet where nobody went because it was disgusting.
Lucy shouted, 'Rose petals!'
Suddenly there was a silvery light and there were thousands of fairies. Lucy became one too and Sarah fainted. She couldn't believe it. It was like being knocked over with your eyes closed.

Sarah woke up and pinched Lucy to see if she was real. Lucy was the rose fairy. Five seconds later Sarah found herself back at the girls' toilets.

Sarah is now Lucy's friend and she doesn't bully her anymore. She does believe in fairies, (but she doesn't tell anyone),

Charlotte Andrasi (10)
Kings Hedges Primary School, Cambridge

THE RAINFOREST

Mia was walking excitedly in the rainforest but she knew there were dangerous animals. It was very humid until the rain tumbled down and Mia ran for shelter. When the rain had stopped Mia was surprised and worried, she didn't recognise where she was.

The harpy eagle is a dangerous animal and he has fierce eyes like a devil. He eats monkeys and other big creatures. He was sitting in a canopy and he spotted Mia. He thought that Mia might make a nice change from his usual food, so he chased her.

Jaguars are normally fierce but this one wasn't. He had glittering golden eyes and his eyelashes were flickering in the light. All of a sudden the jaguar spotted Mia's danger and wanted to help. He sprinted like he had never before. The jaguar then led Mia through the undergrowth but on his way he spotted the eagle ready to eat someone. As the eagle swooped to catch Mia the jaguar saved her.

The good thing about the jaguar is that he knew all the short cuts through the jungle and he realised Mia needed to get back to her tribe quickly.
'Slow down, slow down,' said Mia.
The jaguar kept going at a fast pace.

Half an hour later the jaguar found Mia's tribe but realised he must be careful in case they were afraid of him.

It all turned out well and Mia is now back home with her family and they are all happy and glad.

Madeleine Crofts (10)
Kings Hedges Primary School, Cambridge

A Day In The Life Of Mickey Mouse

Monday 23rd June

Today I woke up and went down my creaky, curly stairs to go and get some yummy breakfast, because I was starving. All of a sudden, just as I sat down, I heard a knock on the door. *Rat-tat-tat!* I thought it was just my letterbox so I carried on eating, but then it happened again.
Rat-tat-tat! I stumbled and got up to see who it was.

It was my friend Minnie with her spotted bow and her spotted dress. She looked so wonderful wearing all the spotted clothes. 'What have you come round for?' I asked.
'Because it is a very special day today,' Minnie explained.
'A very special day for what?' I asked. 'Tell me what the very special day is, I want to know quickly.'

When Minnie told me I said, 'No, it's not my birthday today, or is it. I thought my birthday was tomorrow.'
'No it's definitely today, I've written it in my diary. Have a look!' she said.
I looked and it said, 'Mickey Mouse's birthday - do not forget the present!'

After that she gave me a blue box with yellow spots and a ribbon tied to it. It was a real surprise and a lovely day for me!

Nicola Bailey (10)
Kings Hedges Primary School, Cambridge

A Day In The Life Of Sabrina

It was a sunny day, Sabrina had just moved into a new house. They were just unpacking when her mum had to go out for some food.

When she had gone, Sabrina started to wander around the towering house. When she finally got to the top of the house there was a silver door. She climbed through the door and walked around. It looked just like a normal attic but suddenly the door shut with a *bang!* Sabrina tried to open the door but it just stayed shut. The attic was gloomy and misty. She looked around the room and rummaged through all the dusty boxes.

Sabrina found a very strange old book in one of the boxes. When she opened it a beaming door appeared. Sabrina walked through the door and found herself in a wet, damp place with huge trees, bushes and lots of exotic animals. She realised that she was in the middle of the rainforest. She looked around the astonishing forest but realised that her mum would be back soon.

Sabrina started running and pushing the bushes out of the way. When she spotted the door, she sprinted through it. Then she woke up on her suitcase. She was so frightened and never went up to the attic again!

Jamie-Lee Anderson (10)
Kings Hedges Primary School, Cambridge

A Day In The Life Of Benji

One puppy morning, Julie, Kyle and Jake came downstairs noisily. They came into the kitchen and woke me up just as I was having a lovely dream about bones. Julie unlocked the door and I went outside to the toilet.

I came back inside and Julie and Jake had disappeared somewhere but about five minutes later Julie came back. At about half-eight Kyle and Julie left home. Kyle wasn't looking too happy as I had eaten his homework.

After a long time the whole family came back. Kyle got my lead out of a drawer. I got all excited but I was told to sit still. He put my lead on and we started to walk. We got to a big green near a lot of trees and he let me off my lead. I started to play with Kyle. It was fun - I liked playing with Kyle.

Suddenly I heard a noise in the long grass and out came a big black dog and it started chasing me. 'Help, help! Why can nobody hear me?' I woofed.
Kyle was shouting, 'Come back Benji.' He started to run after the black dog, caught up with him and chased him away.
Phew! I thought. *I'm glad that's over. Thanks Kyle.*

I ran back to Kyle and he put me back on my lead. We walked back home and Kyle told Julie what had happened.

Home sweet home - time for a nap!

Kyle Lavender (10)
Kings Hedges Primary School, Cambridge

THE CHAIN

There she stands, 7ft tall, staring at me. I'm not sure why she's staring at me, maybe it's the chain on my neck.

'My name is Queen Akula and you're coming with me!'
'What do you want with me?' asked Adam.
'You see that chain on your neck, it can do wonderful things. I need your help as our city has been taken over by slugs,' she said.
'Slugs? Ha, they're tiny. Just pour salt over them,' Adam replied.
'Salt? What's salt?' she asked.

* * *

'What is this place?' Adam asked.
'Home,' said Queen Akula. 'As you see, these slugs are not small!'
'OK, can I go home now?' asked Adam. 'Hey, get off me!'
'You're going to the slug king,' said one of the slugs.
'We have intruders. Put them in the dungeon!' commanded the slug king.
'Not the dungeon,' cried Queen Akula. 'Anything but the dungeon!'
'Fine, the guillotine then!'
'No, not the guillotine. Dungeon, dungeon, dungeon!'

'So this is the dungeon,' said Adam. 'There's no way out. Hey what's this in my pocket! Just what we want, a file to cut the bars.'
'We can use these bones to knock out the guards,' explained Queen Akula.
'Good thinking!' said Adam. 'Now where are those slimy slugs.'
'They're in the hall. Follow me,' explained Queen Akula. 'There's no way we can get in.'

My chain is tightening. I should take it off as its turning into a sword. I'll have to fight them alone. I went into the hall and killed every single slug. After that I said goodbye to Queen Akula and went home.

Adam Mayes (10)
Kings Hedges Primary School, Cambridge

A Day In The Life Of Water Snails In My Fish Tank

One bright fish day, I was slurping on the fish tank with my mates, when a big angelfish budged me real hard and I couldn't get my lunch. After that terrible shock, I told my tribe and they were very shocked about the incident, as usually we are all very alert.

We had a discussion as to how we could take revenge on those evil fish and after some time of thinking long and hard, Jazzy had an idea that we should throw stones at the evil fish.

My tribe and I got some light stones and got into position to shoot at the fish. Every stone missed because the fish dodged them. It looked like nothing would stop them.

An idea popped into my head and I told the tribe about it. They thought it was brilliant. We tried my plan, which was to get on the glass again and when the fish bashed us off, we would drop down on their backs. Fish don't like being clung on to.

We got into our positions and one, two, three, we got on their backs. An hour later they asked us to stop clinging onto them. We then made an agreement that if they stopped brushing us off the glass wall, we would stop holding onto them.

Now we are able to slurp in peace.

Gabriel Silva (10)
Kings Hedges Primary School, Cambridge

WHITE WOLVES

'Help! Please help!' Alexander yelled as he was pursued by a pack of ravenous, bloodthirsty, white wolves. He jumped over logs, dodged trees and clambered over hills and rocks. Alexander didn't know where he was off to on an adventure. *It must be because of my stone,* he thought. He was carrying a bold lilac diamond in his pocket.

Alexander ran through the greenery and flung himself up a high oak tree. He grabbed hold of a brittle branch, it snapped and he fell onto the roots of the oak tree. His stone flew from his pocket. The biggest of the white wolves carried it off, turning brown while doing so.

Alexander picked himself up and followed the wolf to a dark cave which was full of white wolves. Alexander ran in, grabbed the lilac rock and fled for the door.

He was stopped by a voice growling, 'Where do you think you're going?' It was the king wolf. 'Give me the stone, you don't know what power it possesses!'
The king wolf then growled something to a nearby wolf and it leapt at him. Others followed and Alexander picked up a long spiky stick and fought them off.

Hours later the king wolf called back his wolves, 'You are willing to do anything for the stone?'
Alexander nodded.
'If you let us use it from time to time, you can keep it and we will be your friends.'
Alexander agreed and stroked the friendly king.

All of the wolves and Alexander were now allied peacefully.

Zoe Mackey (10)
Kings Hedges Primary School, Cambridge

THE GHOST OF MAX WHITE

This story has been handed down in all the pubs in England and is told every thirty-first of October.

The year was 1789 and Max White was panting for breath but he kept on steaming ahead. His feet were searing with pain but he insisted on carrying on. At the moment he was beating his sister Sarah. A crack of thunder signalled the start of rain, so he halted at 12 Avenue Street.

It was either now or never. He could go the safe way or the short cut. He then heard a jingling noise and a *clip-clop, clip-clop*. His brain was whirring and then he decided to go into Thirteenth Avenue. He stopped as he heard a horse and he then closed his eyes. He opened them again and he was fine. He then began running again.

He soon came to the eerie graveyard in the street and opened the rusty gate. The graveyard was very uninviting. Max started running but suddenly he tripped. A cloaked figure grabbed him and knocked him back against the gate. A knife glinted in his belt and the figure reached for it. All the while, whilst the figure was getting his knife, he kept his red, glowing eyes on Max.

The rain lashed down and Max whipped some rain from his cheek but when he saw his hand it was covered in blood. Just then a car zoomed past and the figure pointed to a grave.

Max brushed the dust off and read 'Max White 1778-1789'.

Charlie Bailey (11)
Maidwell Hall School, Northampton

TRAPPED

You can always tell in a zoo which tigers have been taken from the wild and which were bred in captivity. The captured ones have a wild look in their eyes and leap about their cages, forever seeking a way out. You can see their hatred of the human race, their yearning to escape and hunt living flesh, not wanting to be fed by a zookeeper. This is a story about one . . .

A particularly wild tiger had once been free, the wind in his face, the raw power of life coursing through him. He smelt a herd of zebra and stealthily set out through the grass, stopping in a mud bank, perfectly camouflaged against the clay.

The herd was close. In a few minutes he could see them, their black and white forms trudging through the grass. He slipped silently into the grass, barely making a ripple, slipping towards the herd.

Suddenly a jeep came hurtling through the savannah, the ugly monstrous shape almost flying towards the tiger. He did the only thing he could - he ran, his paws slamming so hard that they made dents in the earth. He ran but they caught him. A man shot him with a tranquilliser. The tiger fell immediately.

When he awoke, he found he was in a cage and passing him were many of the same species that had trapped him. He snarled and jumped against the bars, trying to rip at their flesh but he could not. He was trapped.

Robert Newton (10)
Maidwell Hall School, Northampton

ENTER AT YOUR PERIL

At number 42 Orange Street, London, there lived twins called Gregory and Horace. Gregory was ten with short brown hair and green eyes. Horace was ten and had blond hair and blue eyes.

One October they were allowed to go on holiday with their friend Bob to Scotland. When they got to Bob's holiday house they explored the moor around it.

They had been walking for about an hour when Gregory saw a stone arch leading into a cave and on one side Horace saw that there was some writing and it read:
'Those who enter
Must go to the centre
Or doom will appear
And your life you'll fear'.

'That's rubbish,' said Horace. 'I bet there's gold hidden in there and somebody doesn't want us to find it.'
'I'm not sure,' said Bob. 'They say there are ghosts on these moors.'
Gregory spoke, 'Tut! Ghosts are just rubbish and anyway if they're real they can't hurt us. They would just go straight through us.'
'Alright,' gave in Bob, 'but Horace goes in first.'
'Why me?' complained Horace.

Horace started walking towards the door, when he noticed that the others weren't following. He turned and then, shaking with fear, as he turned back again, he saw two large and evil red eyes.
'Run!' Gregory yelled.

They ran and ran until they were home.
'Dad!' yelled Bob. 'We have just seen a creature with huge red eyes...'

Would you have believed them?

Henry Ferrari (9)
Maidwell Hall School, Northampton

THE PHANTOM OF GARNHILL CEMETERY

Thud! A noise rapped against the door of Garnhill Cemetery keeper's cottage. Luigi Tomali woke with a start. Luigi was tall and lanky and had short black hair and an untidy moustache. 'Anybody there?' he asked.

There came a spine-chilling whisper in the darkness, 'I will hunt you. I will kill you!'

Luigi nearly died of fright. He grabbed the poker lying next to the embers of the fire and edged along the corridor and out of the door.

In the graveyard, tombstones littered the stony path, a light breeze blew and the moon was full. At the end of the path stood a horse, black with glowing red eyes. On top of the horse sat a headless rider, clad in black armour. He was wielding a giant battleaxe. As he was moving towards him, Luigi pointed the poker at the headless rider but it was too late. The last thing Luigi remembered was a huge pain in his neck. His head tumbled to the ground. The horseman wasn't seen again until . . .

One Jack Hamilton was walking down that lane and he too saw the spectre. He drew his sword and countered him (Jack happened to be an expert swordsman). The horseman raised his axe and swung down in an 180 degree arc. Jack blocked and stabbed the spectre through, but the blade just passed through him. Jack knew the dead horseman's name, Eric Von Vlacstein. His grave was in the cemetery. Jack knew what to do, as he had heard stories in pubs about this. He stabbed down with all his might into the grave, from then on the horseman vanished.

Matthew Wiley (10)
Maidwell Hall School, Northampton

THEY ARE COMING

Lightning cracked overhead. The rain lashed down on a small building in the middle of a dark forest. A man stood silhouetted against the lightning by a window running the whole length of the building. A small skinnier man, wearing jeans and a white coat come over to him.

'They are coming,' the older man said.
'How do you know?' the skinny man asked.

The older man pointed to one part of the sky, where lots of little purple and white flashes popped up. They grew bigger each time.

The skinny man tugged at the old man's coat, 'Come on, you need some sleep,' he said.

The old man was very reluctant at first but he came over to a desk. The young man asked him how he knew aliens were coming, and the old man told him what he knew.

'I still can't see how you can tell the difference between a rocket and an alien spacecraft,' the young man said.
Then suddenly the older man stood up and leapt on the desk. There was a fizzing noise and the electricity went off. The older man grabbed the younger man by the scruff of the neck. The old man turned to the window and exclaimed, 'They are here.' He took off his mask and revealed he was an alien.

Through the window was a spaceship floating down to Earth. The alien looked menacing with the window silhouetting him. That was the last thing that the man saw. The blue alien face with three purple eyes and a vaporiser in his hand. He came towards him and then . . .

Sebastian Tiley (11)
Maidwell Hall School, Northampton

MY SPECIAL DAY ENDED OK

'Surprise!' Tris woke suddenly, her parents and her brother (Ben) had just woken her up at approximately 7.30am, in front of her was about 12 presents (as it was her birthday). Tris had a gleaming smile on her face...

She sharply got out of bed and started wondering what lovely presents would be inside the wrapping paper. She steadily started ripping the paper off the presents. *Wow!* She got everything she wanted. A new bike, recorder, doll, karaoke machine. Ah! Tris had just realised that her best friend (Teri) was coming round as she was invited to go to the seaside with them.

Bang! Teri was 5 minutes early and Tris was still not dressed.
'Open the door and let Teri in,' shouted Dad (from the upstairs bathroom).
Ben came running to open the door.
'Thank you, you're a star.'
Tris thanked him politely. Teri came in and wondered where Tris was? Ben told her, they started chatting about the seaside. Then they were all ready to go to the seaside. Everyone went in the car with all their luggage. Dad saw there was only one tick of petrol left (not a lot left). 'I will be fine,' he muttered to himself.

They set off and halfway there the petrol had gone, fortunately they were right near a petrol station. Off they went again, but when they got there the seaside was closed. They went back home and had a party there instead of at the seaside.

Rebekah Saunders (11)
Middleton Primary School, Peterborough

THE HOUSE COMMITTED SUICIDE

'Have you finished packing yet?' shouted Jack to Kate.
'Yes,' replied Kate as she slung her black suitcase into the car boot.
'Finally we can go!' cried Simon.

Jack, Simon and Kate had been in the car for hours, they were sweating like pigs.
'How much longer?' asked Kate.
'Ages,' replied Simon.

When they finally got there it was night. The house they were staying in looked haunted, never-the-less the trio went in the house, found a room each and settled down to sleep because they were too tired to unpack.

While they were sleeping there were strange noises which were taking over their minds, so as a result they would see things and believe they were real.

Next morning, Kate, Jack and Simon went out of the house and at that time the noises which were taking over their minds started to affect them.
'Hi,' said a voice.
'I'm Jacqueline,' said Jacqueline looking cheerful.
The three friends turned around.
'I'm going to suck your blood.'
The three friends ran into the car and drove away.

When they got away they climbed on a tall building's roof and then . . . there was a bloody sight.
'Oh no,' shrieked the dead bodies' parents.

Later on the police investigated the deaths of the trio.
'Unfortunately they committed suicide,' said a detective.
'But why?' sobbed the parents.
'We shall never know,' sighed the detective.

After that the parents of the trio remained sad for the rest of their lives.

Jonathan Feltell (11)
Middleton Primary School, Peterborough

THE DEADLY MAN

One dark, cold, gloomy evening sat an old woman called Sue in her lounge watching TV. It was getting very late so Sue turned her TV off and could hear a noise which was like fingers scraping down a blackboard. Sue listened carefully where the noise was coming from, she thought it was coming from the attic but when she went up, nothing was there. She listened again. She thought it would be in the basement. When she got into the basement there was a massive monster which had green eyes, no hair and hairy hands like they belonged to a bear.

'Help!' shouted Sue.
'Shut up!' roared the monster.
Sue quickly ran upstairs and phoned the police.

Half an hour later the police eventually came and Sue shouted,
'Down in the basement.'
The police ran down. When the police got downstairs all that was there was a massive hole in the wall with blood all over the floor.

The police immediately ran upstairs and contacted more police to try to find this deadly man. The weather was getting very noisy with thunder all over the sky.

Soon after, the police could see a man with no head in the distance. The police said, 'Stop walking, turn around and kneel.'
The man knelt down and the police took one shot and he died right in front of Sue.

Matthew Fynn (11)
Middleton Primary School, Peterborough

A DAY IN THE LIFE OF BUFFY

It all started when I was dreaming about being Buffy the Vampire Slayer. However I heard a loud bang. I woke up to see a vampire: white hair, black leather jacket and a scar over his right eye. I found out his name was Spike.

As I got out of bed he said, 'I hear you're Buffy the Vampire Slayer.' 'No, my name is not Buffy,' I said feeling weak. 'I just said that!' I could not bring myself to say my real name.

Spike, the vampire took a swing at me, I fell on the bed, it really hurt. I thought about what the real Buffy would do. I took a lamp and smashed it over his head. I legged it to my friend's house. My friend, Holly said I looked like Buffy, Holly looked like Willow, the real Buffy's friend. We got Ben but he changed to Xander, also Buffy's friend.

It was midnight, we started fighting vampires. We knew where the weapons were, it was like we were really them.

We were at the park sitting on the swings waiting to fight, it was a place that was dangerous, a place where Buffy would be. I bumped into Spike again, I don't know why we weren't fighting but he soon said why, he loves me . . .

Yvonne Jones (11)
Middleton Primary School, Peterborough

THE HOUSE OF NEW RETURN

On the fifth of December 1850, the Lee family were having a party in one of their mansions, Lancaster. The children were snuggled up in bed when Mrs Lee heard a scream. She went to check on them. The window was wide open and the children were gone! *'Aaahhh!'* Everyone went upstairs, no one came down . . .

'Go on, dare you!' sneered Harrison, the darer of Patterson Road. He had just dared John, Pete, Jamie and Harry to go into the abandoned mansion, 'Lancaster' that had been empty for 200 years.
'We'll, go tomorrow.'
'Come on you guys, sooner we get done, sooner we can get out,' ordered John.
'But why? I'd rather be a wimp. stop!' moaned Pete, moping up the old gravel path. They opened the old creaky oak door, *creak* went the door. They went in.

'Ah, help me,' howled Harry but by the time they turned around it was too late. Harry had gone.
'OK, let's search the place top to bottom, with any luck we'll find Harry, let's go!' ordered Pete, sounding calm.
'You haven't seen my torch have you?' stuttered Jamie.
'It was over there . . .' John pointed to what was an empty space but was now covered by rags.
'Let's go!' murmured Pete.

All three got out but Harry was never found. Every full moon you can hear his scream . . .

William Lobley (11)
Middleton Primary School, Peterborough

A Day In The Life Of A Tree

At 9.30am I was awoken by a sharp gust of wind blowing in my direction. *Ho hum, it's the start of a new day,* I thought to myself between large gulps of fresh air. I then realised I had spectators and shut my mouth quickly before those stupid humans discovered that trees have mouths.

At around 11.00 a family of mice decided that my roots would make a perfect home. They didn't even have the manners to ask me. It itched dreadfully, but being a tree, I could do nothing about it.

It was about 12 o'clockish when a human with an orange hard hat got out a chainsaw and switched it on! I knew what that meant and I promptly gave him an almighty *whack!* with my branches and sent him flying. I don't think I'll see him again.

2.30 brought a whole assembly of humans to the meadow. A few tried to climb on me, but as soon as they got up to one of my higher branches, I flung them onto the ground. A big white van pulled up next to the meadow and escorted the humans I flung away, so I was happy.

At 3.30 the humans had gone, so I had a quick snooze. After an hour though I was disturbed, this time by a group of rabbits. They obviously wanted a home in my roots too. By this time I had got used to the itching and I decided to carry on sleeping till dawn.

Grace Summon (11)
Middleton Primary School, Peterborough

DINOSAUR ATTACK

Chapter one

On Saturday morning, Max was munching away on his cereal, when the telephone started ringing. Max's mum shuffled over to the phone. 'Hello, oh hi Roxy, yes I'll just get him for you,' replied Max's mum sweetly.

Max had already scampered over to the phone, before his mum could bellow. Max placed the phone down and resumed eating his Frosties.
'What did Roxy want?' questioned Karen (Max's mum).
'Oh, just to ask if I wanted to go to the museum today,' slurped Max. (He was halfway through eating).
'Well, are you going then?' asked Karen.
'Yeah, I might as well,' answered Max. He clambered upstairs to get ready. When he was ready he scrambled down the path to meet Roxy by a lamp post (as usual).
'Hi, are you ready then?' grinned Roxy. They set off for the museum.

Chapter two

'Have you got your bus fare Max?' exclaimed Roxy.
Max nodded while clutching his change to his chest. They dashed off the bus and stumbled down the stony, steep hill.
'Welcome to Stone Hill Museum, I hope you enjoy your stay,' announced an assistant.

The children smirked and made their way to the model dinosaurs.
'Wow these dinosaur models are breathtaking,' gasped Max.
Roxy disagreed. 'Max I'm sure that dinosaur's eye just twitched,' trembled Roxy.
Max had also noticed something strange about the model. They both stumbled backwards. Suddenly . . . the dinosaur rose. Just then it snapped at the terrified children!

Amy O'Malley (10)
Middleton Primary School, Peterborough

A Day In The Life Of A Mouse In A Holiday Home

It would seem a late start to most, but at 7.00pm, I woke up, thinking how early it was. All seemed quiet - as usual - and as I peeked at my biscuit supply, I realised I was down to the last one. The owners had not visited for months and so I (being a fat fellow) was rapidly losing weight. Unfortunately, they had left the cupboards locked, so I decided I had to move.

I knew I would be welcome in the house opposite, but I didn't want to leave. Regretfully, I began to pack my few belongings. *Bang!* I darted behind the drinks cabinet, just as four unfamiliar people entered the house. A lady had a seemingly heavy bag, which she dragged towards the kitchen and slammed down - where I had been a minute ago.

'Breadsticks for supper,' she exclaimed. The children groaned and went off, sulking. By then, I was trembling excitedly. Food! A man sliced the bread and took it to the table. My greedy eyes noticed he had left some crumbs. Without hesitation, I ran out and began nibbling.

I was happily munching when he returned, paused, grabbed his glasses case and angrily struck the bread, narrowly missing my head. I leapt towards the wall and soared through a hole, through the air and landed in front of a vicious black cat. Quickening my pace, I reluctantly ran to the house opposite. The door was ajar and I sprinted through it. Safe at last - for now . . .

Abigail Sykes (10)
Middleton Primary School, Peterborough

THE CHINESE MYSTERY

It was 5.00am, everything was silent, when suddenly Matthew's waterbed *exploded*. Danny and Ryan were absolutely soaked. They jumped up and pounded Matthew with their pillows.

Danny and Ryan changed out of their soaking wet clothes and went outside. Ryan filled up the water pistol, pulled the trigger and soaked Matt. Suddenly Danny tripped over a black bag. 'Who put that there?' Danny said angrily. He took a peep inside; there was a box, slightly burnt on each corner.
'Look!' they said in amazement. 'What is in it?'
Danny opened the box and there was a baby's shoe, a flower, one flip-flop, three chopsticks, a box inside a box, then a bag with nail varnish in it and a photograph. Ryan remembered seeing these items in the Chinese restaurant.
'This is a mystery we'll have to solve.'

Danny said, 'Let's go and see the restaurant owner.' The door was open and they went inside. The room was pitch black. They switched on their torches and looked around. They were surprised to see the caravan owner and the Chinese restaurant owner lying unconscious on the floor. Matthew dragged them into a cupboard and locked the door. Ryan phoned the police and when they arrived they were very pleased. 'We've been looking for two thieves for a long time and you three have solved the mystery.'

The boys were given a reward of £300,000 each. 'What a holiday, we can afford to buy our own hotel now,' they all agreed.

Danny Mills & Ryan Manning (11)
Middleton Primary School, Peterborough

POWERS

On the highest mountain in the darkest town lived a small girl. She wasn't any ordinary girl, she had evil powers which she hated.

Right now I bet you're thinking you would love to have evil powers. However these powers make you as nasty as can be. In addition only a witch/evil creature can use them. Zoe (the keeper of the powers) is not evil so she can't use them in any way.

Zoe's mission is to get rid of the powers, but I bet to be honest her chances are slim. She might not get rid of the powers.

Bang! Bang! went a horrible noise. The noise went again. The noise was someone knocking at a door. Zoe heard no reply so she opened the door that she continuously knocked at. The air was silent in the house. In a little room Zoe asked an old lady about the powers. The old lady was nasty and perfect for the transformation (she wouldn't change a bit). The lady agreed to the deal and waited for the bottle of evil to come to her until *smash!* the bottle of evil dropped out of Zoe's tender hands and hit the floor. Evil spread everywhere.

Beware of the evil ant!

Chantelle Cox (11)
Middleton Primary School, Peterborough

ALLEREDNIC

Once upon a time in a far away castle, there was a princess named Allerednic. Unfortunately she was beset by a dragon, put there by Estress, a wicked witch.

'Oh I wish a charming, handsome prince would whisk me off my feet and out of the window, but until then all I can do is dream.' Allerednic sighed as she turned towards the window and peered out into the dark starry night.

Meanwhile, two hundred miles away, Prince Janeson was just waking up. He was thinking about a decision that could change his whole life. He wanted a wife. He announced this at breakfast to his family and immediately went to find the princess of his dreams.

He searched north, south, east and west and still could not find his future wife until a glistening light caught his eye. It was the castle where Princess Allerednic was imprisoned. He set off towards the castle at once on his noble white stallion.

Alone he crept into the castle not knowing what danger lie ahead. A loud roar made him come to a halt. Janeson looked around but there was nothing in sight. Then he looked up. There it was, a fire-breathing dragon.

Janeson battle the dragon for over an hour. He thrust his sword into the dragon and ended the battle with an almighty swing. Then he ran to the tallest tower to find Princess Allerednic.

Janeson brought her back to the palace and they lived happily ever after!

Maxine Taylor (11)
Middleton Primary School, Peterborough

THE HAUNTED HOUSE

'Zoë, come here,' shouted Hannah kicking Zoë's door.
'I'll come out if you stop kicking my door,' replied Zoë.
Quickly Hannah stopped and the door swung open. 'Zoë, I've got a scary adventure for us!'
'Where?'
'At the haunted house in the next block.'
'Let's go!'

Ten minutes later they were at the haunted house. *Creak, bang,* the door closed and they were in the creepy dark hall. They walked slowly up the stairs and then they saw a ghostly white ghost and a witch having a conversation, so carefully and very quietly they crept near them and listened.
'Guster, we need children to come to this house, I'm starving with hunger!' cried the witch.
'Well, Wicked, you're a witch, you can turn into a child's friend and bring them here.'
'Yes, I can, can't I. Wait there, I can smell a child. Let's go and look.'

Quickly Zoë and Hannah ran downstairs to the nearest room. While they were scared, hiding, Wicked and Guster started looking around.
'Wicked, where are they? Can you see if your nose can find them?'
'I'll try,' Wicked replied.

Off Wicked went, smelling everywhere, while Guster followed close behind. Finally they got to the room where Hannah and Zoë were and quietly crept up to them, but waiting for the right moment. While the witch and ghost were waiting the two girls stayed still and very quiet. When suddenly . . .

Wicked and Guster stabbed the girls. From then on no one went in there again.

Emma Cattermoul (10)
Middleton Primary School, Peterborough

BOYFRIEND HORROR

Hi, I'm Bethany and I am going to tell you a story to make your boyfriends look perfect.

It started on a cold blustery morning. I woke with a smile on my face (I don't know why though) although when I looked out of the window my smile disappeared. *Ring! Ring!* went the phone when I was pulling down my bed trousers and putting on my tights. 'Bethany, it's for you, darling,' bellowed my mum from downstairs. I ran down the stairs with my grey tights hanging from my legs.

It was Rosy (one of my friends). This is what she said, 'Hi Beth, are you doing anything on Friday night?'
I answered, 'No.'
'Can you sleep then?'
I jumped up straight away and asked my mum, of course she said yes.

The day came quickly, however it was exciting. When I got home from school my mum was upstairs packing my stuff.
'Mummy, I'm home.'
I heard a rustling upstairs. I assumed it was my mum. It was.
'Hi darling, I'm packing for you!'

I was finally at her door. It opened and I went in. We played with our make-up and jewellery. However something terrible happened!

Ring, ring went their phone; we listened.
'Hello is Rosy there?' said the voice. It was Darren, my boyfriend! I got into an argument, Darren was a two-timer. I dumped him straight away, so did Rosy.

April Cole (10)
Middleton Primary School, Peterborough

JACK AND THE EVIL GOBLIN

In November 1999, there was a boy called Jack. In the lush green garden he was feeding his animals when suddenly a red thing sped past, he saw it and flinched.

The next morning Jack went to school. Whilst he was crossing the road he heard a squeaky laugh, a goblin was peeking at him through the bush, then he walked to the school bus.

When Jack was on the bus he looked out of the window. There it was, the goblin. He recognised that voice and its head and face. The goblin pulled out a knife, went round the front and stabbed the driver who fainted. The bus was out of control, everybody was screaming and shouting. Suddenly the bus careered off the edge of the road and crashed into a ditch. Meanwhile the goblin went round the side of the bus where the boy was sitting. Jack let out another scream and went out of the back of the bus.

Jack was frantic and went running through the woods with the goblin following him. Whilst he was running he fell down a ditch and the goblin had him cornered. But Jack was quick and climbed out. Jack went running to the bus and hid inside. The goblin pulled out a rocket launcher, he fired the launcher with incredible force and blew up the bus with Jack hiding inside. Could the force of the blast have killed Jack?

Adam Burnham (11)
Middleton Primary School, Peterborough

CURIOUS BOYS

Boom! went the thunder. 'I'm scared. It's really creepy in here and so cold!' cried Freddy.

'Yeah, I hate Vince and his friends for daring us to go in here. I can't wait to get him back. I'm thinking about spiders, do you agree?' plotted Victor, a youthful twin boy who was searching the house for a dare.

'Arghhh!' screeched something, to the children's horror it was a zombie, it had robust arms with nimble feet and eyes that were half hanging out of his eye sockets and slime dripping from his arms and face.

Unable to speak, Victor and Freddy started to run as fast as their legs could take them, not once looking back. Eventually the boys worked their way into a cul-de-sac with a small alcove, the boys were trapped for sure. They ran into a corner with closed eyes.

Thump! The zombie hit his head on the slope and fell to the ground, the children took advantage of this mistake and kicked the zombie in the head, bringing the zombie to its death. The children scurried out of the house and ran to safety.

'I'm glad we're safe again. I can assure you that I'm not going in there again,' said a relieved Victor.
'Arghhh! Help me Victor!'

Ryan Howden (11)
Middleton Primary School, Peterborough

THE TEMPLE OF DEMONS

In the midst of India where a sacred temple remains, there is a legend of a demon looking for revenge on a man who destroyed him years ago.

The grandson of the man was standing in front of the temple, his heart beating like a drum, not knowing what was to come.

He entered the temple of demons, there were cobwebs in every corner. The grandson (David) walked at least 8 metres until he heard banging on the wall. David walked up the winding staircase, the banging following - there was still no sign of the demon.

That was when David realised it travelled through the walls - he couldn't destroy it until it came from the steel barricade. The pain in David's back became unbearable as it started to wear him down so he stopped. The banging stopped along with him.

However, the silence was broken by a creature breathing with sorrow. As David turned round he couldn't believe his eyes. It was his grandad's very own dog! It had been so long since they had seen each other, David had forgotten his name. Suddenly the dog squealed, David turned again sniffly . . . the dog was dead! Then the demon attacked David, although David fought back by getting a sword and chopping off its head!

He ran out of the sacred temple and the demon never troubled anyone ever again, or would he arise once again?

Daniel Bailey (11)
Middleton Primary School, Peterborough

SUFFERING FOR SURVIVAL

It was a sad, long day after Trudy's parents had died from a disastrous car crash; when she decided to move in with her best friend's family.

Trudy and Shree were asked to go to the shop where they saw a slimy, sparkly piece of paper glaring out of the drain. They couldn't believe their eyes, they saw two cruise tickets untouched lying there halfway in the drain, they were delighted with joy.

Finally the moment came to depart on a ginormous ferry but as soon as they were in the middle of the ocean they felt the ferry shaking harder every second and they discovered that the ferry was going to sink.

As the ferry was sinking they barged their way through the frightened and terrified crowd; to get to the very last lifeboat specially made for two.

Eventually they arrived at land and for no reason wrote SOS, not knowing what it meant.

Unexpectedly an aeroplane passed by and saw in bold seaweed letters, SOS. '1, 2, 3 over, two little girls stuck on a desert island.'

At last they were rescued and rushed to the hospital suffering from serious flu, but will they survive?

Hannah Stannard (11)
Middleton Primary School, Peterborough

DAVID BECKHAM

Hi, I'm David Beckham and the year is 2028. I've retired from playing football because I'm too old, but my eldest son, Brooklyn, is playing for England against Germany.

Meanwhile, my other son, Romeo, has followed Victoria, my ex-wife, and now he's a pop star. He's living a life of luxury with a beautiful girlfriend called Juliet.

As you might not know this, Victoria and I are divorced, and now I'm married to a lovely lady, Christina Aguilera, and if I play a little game of footie with Brooklyn and get muddy, then she sings her favourite song, 'Dirrty'. Also, if we watch a video, we normally watch 'Aladdin' and she sings 'Genie in a Bottle'!

Anyway, enough of that. About my ex-wife, we had an argument about who was the best footballer and I said I was, so I said that I'd prove it. I curled it into the top corner of the goal and the net ripped. Well, that's what I thought I did, but I actually curled Victoria into the top corner of the window and the glass smashed. The ambulance arrived and said she was going to casualty and Victoria got the wrong idea and made her hair really nice, because she thought she was going to be on telly.

That is what happened to my ex-wife, but now she's fine (unfortunately) and singing as badly as she used to. And she's living a lovely life with none other than Sir Alex Ferguson!

Chris Porter (10)
Orton Wistow Primary School, Peterborough

THE WITCH'S POTION

It was Friday 13th and was a dark night. Sophie and Ben kept hearing noises. They both climbed out of their bedroom window, still wearing their pyjamas and ran through the woods until they came to a house.

Ben saw some stairs going up to the roof. 'Come on, let's see what's at the top,' Ben said. When they reached the top of the long, winding stairs, there was a window.
'Can you hear voices?' Sophie asked.
'Yes, look there's witches!' he replied.

There were three witches; one dressed in red, one in green and one in violet. They were waving their hands over the cauldron, their long black fingernails nearly as long as their fingers. They were now saying, 'Hocus pocus, make this atrocious,' over the green, bubbly potion.

Ben tripped over a plank of wood and hit his head on the window. 'Ouch!' he screamed.
The three witches looked up and saw them. 'Get those children!' one of them cried.

They ran back down the stairs, and as the witches came out of the front door, they caught them. They grabbed them so tight they couldn't move a finger. They took them in and tied them up. They took a big spoon of the potion and one of the witches opened Sophie's mouth. She screamed and closed it shut.

Sophie and Ben's parents heard screaming and came to find them and took them home safely.

Grace Mills (11)
Orton Wistow Primary School, Peterborough

INTRUDER

The ghost of Rose House had been haunting the same house for two hundred years. Nobody had been inside the house since it became haunted. Helen was the first person to try it in hundreds of years. She was twenty-one, had ginger hair, her eyes were bright green and she didn't believe in ghosts.

The ghost was not very pleased about Helen coming to his house. He had not seen anyone in a hundred years and had forgotten what they looked like, so Helen looked very strange.

The ghost was hovering about one metre off the floor in an unused room. It was thinking. The clock struck midnight. 'That's it!' it said. 'Everyone runs when a ghost starts howling!'
So the ghost slipped through the wall into Helen's bedroom.

The howling was horrible. Several of the neighbours woke up because of the racket, but still Helen didn't wake, because every night she inserted ear plugs. The ghost howled in fury, tearing round the room and turning the lights on and off.

Helen opened her eyes. 'A rat!' she screamed. 'A rat, a rat!' She jumped to her feet, pushed a rat off her bed and ran from the room screaming, 'I'm moving out! I'm going! This place is crawling with rats!'

A grin spread across the ghost's face. She was gone. The ghost that lived in Rose House was alone again.

Sarah Arthur (11)
Orton Wistow Primary School, Peterborough

A Big Mistake

Being a witch isn't easy, especially when you've got an enemy who knows you're not normal . . .

I am totally fed up with mortal schools. My enemy, Libby Smith, always picks on me, saying I'm not normal and stuff. Just last Monday I decided that I had had enough, so I did something really awful to her, that bad that it made me lose my powers for a year! But I don't regret it one bit.

It started when I was in class, sitting on a desk next to Libby Smith. She always acts good in front of teachers, so never embarrasses me in class. I felt I needed the toilet so walked out of the room to go. Libby followed.
'Oh look, weird girl is sneaking out,' Libby screeched.
It was then I realised I had had enough. 'Now I have had enough of trying to play tough, this spell is nasty and it will hurt when it turns you into dirt!' I sang the spell.
There was a sudden *puff* and lying on the floor was a small pile of dirt. I poured it into a jar and took it home to show my aunt.

I shall always remember that day and my powers should be back now. I think I'll go downstairs now and change Libby back to her normal self.

I got downstairs and was about to change Libby back, but my powers wouldn't work for years to come and Libby would stay dirt for years.

Natalie Mackle (11)
Orton Wistow Primary School, Peterborough

THE TERRIFYING MANSION

Mark and Andrew were excited, they thought it would be fun; they were going into a haunted mansion. They both pushed the door and went inside.

Andrew said, 'Let's steal some stuff.' So they looked upstairs and downstairs but they still found nothing, but then they saw a crystal ball. Mark ran to get the crystal ball, when a zombie dragon came out and it started to chase them. Mark and Andrew ran upstairs into the attic and closed the door.

Mark and Andrew got a book about zombies and it showed that zombies are killed in sunlight, so Mark and Andrew ran downstairs and the zombie was at the door. Mark and Andrew ran past the zombie and locked the door. They had both learnt their lesson.

Craig Chalmers (11)
Orton Wistow Primary School, Peterborough

THE TALE OF THE UNDEAD

Sally was always suspicious of her Aunt Louisa, but what she found out that weekend was definitely not what she was expecting!

Sally was sent round to her aunt's. There weren't any neighbours; the tall mansion stood alone, creaking in the mist. It always seemed so foggy there. As you looked out of the battered window, you couldn't see anything.

Sally rang the doorbell and the door squeaked as it swung itself open. As Sally stepped into the old house, she saw her aunt gliding down the stairs. She was so light on her feet it was like she was floating.
'Hello dear, make yourself at home. Your room is the third floor, second on the left.' And *she* left.

Sally was about to go upstairs, when she noticed a door under the radiator. Checking no one was watching, she slipped through. She soon wished she hadn't, for hanging up on a wall was a thin, old skeleton, its glowing red eyes glaring at her. She ran out screaming, only to find her aunt waiting.
'I thought you'd find it eventually. Come and get a drink,' her aunt said. Sally obediently followed, trembling. She couldn't drink, her teeth clinked against the glass.
'It's hard for me, but just remember I love you, no matter what. Now that skeleton you saw, it was mine. My soul lives through it. This must never leave this house.'
'I won't tell!'
'I can't be sure, so I can't let you leave. At least, not alive.'

Helen Walden (10)
Orton Wistow Primary School, Peterborough

DOLLY GIVES BIRTH

One morning, Susie was grooming Dolly when a bird flew into the stable and fluttered around Dolly's head. She didn't like it, so she bucked hard. Dolly broke free and galloped around the yard.

When Dolly was back in her stable and everyone had settled back down, Susie began to notice something wrong with Dolly. She expected it was just the fact that Dolly was old and thought nothing of it.

In the morning when Susie woke up, she had her breakfast, cleaned her teeth and got dressed, then she went outside to see Dolly. When she got outside, she saw Dolly lying down. Susie ran over to her and thought that something had to be wrong. She raced back to the house and shouted for her mum and dad. When they came out, they saw Dolly and called the vet.

The vet came straight away and checked Dolly over.
'I have some good news, Mr and Mrs Lockle, Dolly is going to give birth!'
Susie gasped, the whole family gasped; they were going to get a foal!
'When will she be giving birth?' Dad asked.
'Well, I'm quite prepared to scan her now if you like,' the vet said.
'Thank you,' Mum breathed.

The tests showed Dolly was going to give birth very soon. The vet said that she was probably going to give birth that day.

Dolly gave birth to a baby foal called Swift.
'Isn't she sweet?' Susie cried out in happiness, and everyone agreed.

Antonia Collison (10)
Orton Wistow Primary School, Peterborough

THE DISAPPEARING CAKE

On the 1st December 1991, there lived a boy in a crooked house sitting on a steep hill. The boy's name was Jake and he lived with his mum and dad.

That day, Jake had a party and he invited all his friends to the party. A while later, Jake's mum and dad brought in a birthday cake. His mum said, 'Let's go outside for a bit, then we can eat the cake.'

Then they came inside and were shocked by what they saw.
'The cake has gone,' said Dad in shock.
They rushed round the house looking for the missing cake. An hour later, there was still no sign of the cake. Now the children were starving with hunger. They stopped at 6 past 10, and they had been looking for the sticky cake for hours. They were tired and hungry and they never found the cake again.

Lee Bearley (11)
Orton Wistow Primary School, Peterborough

THE JUNGLE

This is a story that not a lot of people would believe. It happened about one week ago in my house.

'What's that?' I said to myself. 'It's coming from the wardrobe.' So I walked closer. There was a flashing light coming from inside it. I stepped into it and everything went black.

Suddenly, I vanished into a deserted jungle. I was lost, there was nowhere to go, so I searched the jungle for someone. I couldn't find anyone, but then I heard a noise. *Bang, bang, bang!*

I started digging in the ground. It took a long time, but when it was done, there was a coffin. I opened it and there was a tall, old, white-haired man.
He said to me, 'Thank you, I've been in here for so long now. How can I reward you? You can have one wish, and make it good.'
I thought to myself, then said, 'All I want is to go home.'
So he flashed his wand and I was back at home on my bed.

Sean Watson (11)
Orton Wistow Primary School, Peterborough

A Boy's Dream

Hi, I'm Rob Doyle. I'm 11 years old and I'm small and skinny. I have ginger hair and my dream is to play for Everton FC. I want to play for the school team, but bully Oliver Johnson stands in the way of my Everton dream.

Monday morning is school football practice. I'm trying to get in the school team - I've been waiting for this day.
'Rob, darling, breakfast's ready.'
'OK Mum.'
That's my mum, Liverpool mad. She doesn't approve of my Everton dream.
'Hello Mum.'
'Hello darling, eat your breakfast; you're late.'
'Damn, I need my boots.'
'What boots? Sorry, I sold them yesterday.'
'You sold my boots? *Mum!*'
'I'm sorry.'
'Sorry's not good enough. I hate you! I'll never get in the team with no boots.'

'Hello young boy, what's the matter?'
'I've got no boots for practice.'
'Here you go, you have now.'
'Wicked! Football's in five minutes.'

'Rob Doyle, are you playing?'
'Yes.'
'Get your boots on.'
'Oliver Johnson, pass it here, score if you're that good!'

Rob smacks the ball and it flies to the top corner. Rob is granted captain of the school team' his wish of playing for Everton becomes true. The old lady that gave him the boots is rewarded with living with Rob Doyle and his mum for the rest of her life.

Robert Doyle (12)
Orton Wistow Primary School, Peterborough

ONE SCARY DAY

One morning, John was all excited about going to a funfair with his brother, Lee. They both got changed and set off towards the fair.

When they arrived, the fair was already going. There was music blaring from the speakers, roller coasters whizzing around the track. They only had five tickets each.

When they only had one ticket left each, John shouted, 'Let's go on the ghost train, it's great fun.'
So they got in a carriage and went around the track. Lee started to cry and he was saying, 'I want to get off.'
John just laughed out loud. 'Don't worry, it's all made up.'
'Let's go home now then, shall we?'

They were on their way home when a zombie and a lizard jumped out of a bush and grabbed them both and put them to the floor.
'Get off me!' they shouted.
John and Lee kicked them off and ran, the ghost followed them all the way home. They got a shower and sighed in relief.

That night, they were watching TV and all of a sudden, *knock, knock* at the door. Oh no, who could that be?

Michael Wright (11)
Orton Wistow Primary School, Peterborough

THE GHOST TRAIN

Natalie and Michael were at the fair in Manchester. Natalie wanted to go on the ghost train, Michael was not so sure.
'Come on!' repeated Natalie.
Michael soon gave in. 'OK,' whimpered Michael.
As soon as you could say 'zombie', Natalie had gone, dragging Michael along beside her.
'Any more for the ghost train!' shouted the owner. But no more people came.

The train started. Michael got even more scared. The train stopped.
'W-w-w-what's happened?' whispered Michael.
'I think it's broken, just stay calm. Let's get out and explore.'
'OK,' said Michael, worriedly.
'*Wow,* it's a vampire and he's . . .'
'Hello.'
'*Real!*' screamed Natalie.
He picked Michael and gobbled him down in one gulp. 'Umm, tasty, I wonder if you taste the same. Well, we'll have to see.'
'Don't! Help, please help.'

The train started to move again. He froze, so she clambered out of his arms and ran and jumped on the train, but then she woke up drenched in sweat and found it was a dream.

Natalie Edwards (11)
Orton Wistow Primary School, Peterborough

THE DAY I WAS AN ALIEN

I walked up to bed on Friday night, I climbed into my bed and went to sleep.

The next morning I woke up and *aarrghhh!* I was an alien. Then suddenly I was sucked into a vortex and transported to another dimension.

I woke up and I was on a strange planet; everything was red.
'Welcome to the planet Mars.'
'What, I'm not on Earth?'
'Earth, I hate that planet! I'm Zorg and this is my brother Zog. We are planning to take over planet Earth.'
'No you can't! Please don't.'

I was terrified, then I had a sudden determination to save planet Earth. I looked around and found a hole that turned aliens into humans. I jumped through it and I was a human again. I got my penknife and cut the wires of the mothership.

The next thing I knew, I was lying in my bed.

Matthew McKee (11)
Orton Wistow Primary School, Peterborough

VAMPIRES

One gloomy night, there were two boys. Their names were Max and Joe. Max and Joe were going to camp with their school, but then they had the wrong directions and they did not know what to do. Max saw something at the end of the woods, so they went to see what it was; a haunted house.

Max and Joe went inside. It was dark, but they could see a little bit. Then Joe heard a noise. It was coming from the kitchen. It was crashing noises. They went to see what it was.

They saw an eye. It was a vampire. Blood was pouring from his mouth. He had a big cut on his arm - blood was pouring from there as well. So then the vampire picked up a knife and swung it. It cut Max on the arm and it was bleeding very badly, so Max and Joe ran quickly. They had nowhere to go, so Max picked up a knife, swung it, cut the vampire's eye off and he collapsed on the floor. But then he woke up. Then Max got the knife and swung it again. The vampire died.

So then Max and Joe went back home and never came back.

Verinder Sander (10)
Orton Wistow Primary School, Peterborough

SPIDER ATTACK

Can you keep a secret, because I haven't ever told anyone this story before? You are the first to hear it.

In the town of Waggle, a barrel of toxic waste was knocked into a pond outside Sven the scientist's hut. He fed his spiders; they immediately grew to ten times their size and killed Sven.

Meanwhile, Joe's sister was motorcycling with her boyfriend Matt, there was a hole in the wall and two spider tracks; one towards the mall and the other towards the bike track. Joe ran all the way home and told the police. It was too late. One spider was chasing them down the road and the police gathered up to kill the spider. As it came down the road, they shot it about fifty times, it groaned in an extremely deep tone and froze.

Then, they were off to the new mall, where another spider was. They then demolished the other spider, but they found the owner trying to get budget cuts, so everyone had rubbish things, but he didn't know that the mall was smashed and out of business.

Alex Wilde (11)
Orton Wistow Primary School, Peterborough

THE RACE

It was 6am. Eddy was up making breakfast for him and his friends, Eric and Chris. There was a tap and a clunk coming from the front door. Eddy walked over to the door and opened it. There was a fumed smell in the air, the smell of New York. Eddy shut the door and peered down. On the floor was a letter that read: 'You have been selected to take part in a race that goes from the airport to Italy at 7am tomorrow'.

The next morning, Eddy arrived at the airport. There were 49 other cars on the abandoned 30 mile stretch of motorway. Eddy clambered into his car, a Porsche Carerra GT, with Eric and Chris cheering him on. A man on the verge of the road raised his hand, then dropped it, and they were off.

After about 45 minutes of 200mph+ racing, Eddy pulled in with the rest of the pack to a dockyard and boarded a ferry, in sixth place.

When the now 46 remaining cars arrived in Italy, they quickly picked up speed on a public motorway. After about five miles, seven cars had already crashed and Eddy was living dangerously too. There were two miles to the end and Eddy was second. The Ferrari in front suddenly span off. Eddy sped up and won the race.

Eddy got out of his car and was handed a gold cup.

Ross Weatherburn (11)
Orton Wistow Primary School, Peterborough

THE CREEPER

'Mum, can we go out to play?' Rachel asked.
'All right, but be careful,' their mum replied.

Rachel and Michael ran outside, but then suddenly out of the corner of Rachel's eye, she saw a man, but no ordinary man. A man who had a hunched back, who wore green baggy clothes and had brown hair and big, glaring eyes.
'Look!' Rachel whispered. 'Come on, let's follow him.'
'Do we have to?' Michael whined.
'Yes!' she replied.

They tiptoed behind him and they came to a creepy house. They opened the door and started to look around, then they came to a room with a light on. They opened the door to find a man right in front of them. They ran all over the house looking for a place to hide. They ran through rooms, panicking as they ran.

Then suddenly, they found they were trapped in a corner with the man standing on front of the saying, 'Creeper, creeper.' They tried to get away, but they couldn't. They were trapped and nobody saw them ever again.

Alice Chegwidden (11)
Orton Wistow Primary School, Peterborough

THE THIEF

'Hey John!' Jim called, 'Someone's escaped from prison . . . again.'
'So?' said Jim. 'We're still going to the crown jewels festival, I mean, he can't do anything to stop us, can he? He's not exactly gonna steal the crown jewels, is he?'
John and Jim got into their dad's car, and then their dad started the car and headed for the festival.
'C'mon Dad, hurry up. I'm bored,' moaned Jim.
'So am I,' his dad muttered under his breath.
When they finally arrived at the festival, it was just about to start.
'Phew, made it.'

The guards were standing around the jewels and everyone was gazing at them, then the Queen appeared. Instantly, everyone turned to look at her except one guard, who took a bag out of his pocket and slid the crown jewels silently into it. He thought no one would see him, but Jim, who was standing behind him, did see him.
'Hey, he's stealing the crown jewels!' exclaimed Jim. There was an uproar and the thief rant to his Ferrari ENZO and zoomed off.
'Follow me,' said a man with a blank voice. They followed him into his Jaguar XJ220 and then zoomed off after the thief.
'W-wait . . . who are you?' asked John.
'I'm a spy,' he said in the same blank tone.

They found the thief at the airport, trying to sneak onto a plane and after a little struggle, arrested him.
'Now he'll go back to prison, where he belongs.'

Elliot Rippon (11)
Orton Wistow Primary School, Peterborough

THE STRANGEST DAY AT SCHOOL

One morning when I went to school, Mrs Waltop was standing at the gate. She was calling us all towards her.
'Come along, hurry up, we haven't got all day, you know.'
'What's this all about Miss?' Amy asked.
'I'm pleased to tell you we have a new had teacher. His name is Mr Gundi.'
'Can we go in now Miss, before we get told off by our class teacher?' Jemma asked.
'Today we have assembly, then I need all the Year 6s together.'

'Hello children, I'm your new head teacher.'
'Why were you named Mr Gundi?'
'You are very sleepy, you are very sleepy, when you wake up you will be in a maths lesson.'

'Have we been asleep, as it seems that four hours have passed without us doing anything?'
'Do you like our new teacher?'
'He's the best headmaster ever.'
'Guess what, you lot?'
'What?'
'It's home time!'
'What are you on about? It's only 15:03.'
'Oh right, but I got told we were leaving at 15:05.'
So we left and headed home.

'Mum, we've got a new head teacher and he hypnotises you.'
'Stop joking.'
'I'm not.'
'Night, Mum.'
'Night, sweetheart.'

Emma Taylor (11)
Orton Wistow Primary School, Peterborough

THE STAIRS

It was the strangest day of my life . . .

It was an ordinary day to start with, until my mum asked me to get the paint from the attic.

'Sharna, I'm going to paint the hallway. Fetch me the purple paint please.'

I clambered up the dusty wooden stairs, my blonde curls bouncing like a kangaroo. But as I walked further and further, my curls straightened and I froze. I'd been walking for hours and hours. *Maybe there's no end to them,* I thought to myself. I screamed, hoping that somebody would hear me, but it didn't work. I was stuck there forever. What if nobody ever found me? I'd probably die of hunger.

I carried on going as I though I was exaggerating a bit, but I was right, the stairs didn't end! I decided to go back down and then go back up, as I thought the stairs would go back to normal, but of course I was wrong. I got to the fifty-sixth stair, sat down and cried. I hoped that my mum would come, but unfortunately she didn't, which made me even worse.

Eventually I fell asleep and I had a dream that I was stuck on the stairs, so I tapped on the wall three times and suddenly I woke up. I tapped on the wall three times and miraculously, I was at the top of the stairs. 'Sharna, have you got the paint?'

It was the strangest day of my life!

Bethany Becconsall (11)
Orton Wistow Primary School, Peterborough

THE HUNT FOR THE LOST TREASURE

One bright, sunny morning, Amy and Tom set off in search of some treasure.
'Come on Amy, let's go!' shouted Tom excitedly.
Tom and Amy set off to find Beautiful Bay.

Finally they found it. The sand was a golden colour and the sea sounded like maracas being shaken up and down. The sun was as warm as a fire. Amy and Tom thought they had found the spot where the treasure was, so they started to dig.

Tom and Amy were fed up with digging for the treasure, so they decided to go for a walk along the beach. Suddenly, Tom saw something. He thought it was a monkey, but it was a man. He was wearing a yellow T-shirt, beige shorts, brown sandals, a pocket knife and hat. Tom walked up to the man and asked for his name, but he just said,
'What are you up to?'
Tom and Amy didn't understand what he meant and they saw the treasure box at his feet. It was the one they had been looking for all morning. Tom asked the man if he could have the treasure box.
The man said, 'Yes, but on one condition only. If you give me the most valuable piece of jewellery.'
Tom said, 'Yes.'

Tom gave the man the most valuable piece of jewellery, which was a crown with initials engraved on it. Tom and Amy thanked the man and went home for tea.

Rachel Freemantle (11)
Orton Wistow Primary School, Peterborough

THEME PARK

In the foggy, misty distance, stood a little girl called Natalie. She was at an everlasting theme park. It was *enormous* and took up half of England's land.

Natalie took a long walk every Saturday afternoon, although she *still* hadn't finished every single ride at this theme park. Right that minute, Natalie was gradually stepping closer to the Turn Top ride. She wasn't too sure at first about going on the Turn Top ride, but her mum and dad reassured her. She crept towards the ride, even though something did not sound quite right. It suddenly tipped upside down.

The man who controlled the ride, his eyes lit like fire as soon as the ride broke. He asked a tall, fat, tanned man to help him mend the ride. That moment, Natalie got up and stomped out of the theme park and ever since, no one has seen her.

Ellis Bunn (11)
Orton Wistow Primary School, Peterborough

THE LONELY HOUSE

'Wow!' said Matthew to Peter, his best friend in the whole world. Matthew was a boy of muscle and had brilliant brown eyes and bright blond hair. Peter had jet-black hair and green eyes like a green meadow, and a slight off course nose. 'I always wanted to go on an adventure,' Matthew told Peter.
'Up to bed now, you two!' shouted Matthew's mum, so they climbed up the stairs and jumped into their beds and got to sleep.

The next day, Matthew was woken by the sunlight of the morning and Peter had gone. Matthew shouted for his mum and dad, again and again, but no reply. Then *creak.* 'Who's there? Hello?'
'Hello,' and old, misty, sly voice cried. 'I'm called Freddy Kreuger and I'm going to kill you. *Muhahahahaha!*' he bellowed.
Matthew ran around shouting and screaming for help, but on one heard him.

Suddenly, he thought of a plan. He ran straight for the basement door and slammed it shut in front of Freddy Kreuger's face, which got him very mad and angry. Then Matthew sneaked to the secret door and jumped into the air and kicked Freddy Kreuger in the face, he fell into the basement and Matthew locked the door. Then he went to look for his mum and dad. He found Peter in the bathroom and then called the police.

About a week later, Matthew's mum and dad gave Matthew a thank you party.

Jake Gauder (11)
Orton Wistow Primary School, Peterborough

A Night To Remember

This is a story that I have never told anyone before. It's a really strange story and I don't think you will believe me.

One night, I went to sleep. I woke up outside a castle. This castle was enormous; it had two big lookout towers and an old, big, brown door. It looked like it was from the 16th century. I pushed the door with all my might and eventually it slowly opened. I wandered on and found the stairs. They circled up to the lookout tower. I thought to myself, *why is there no one around?*

I saw something shimmering in the distance. I started running, then this man jumped out of nowhere and started chasing me around the castle. I ran into different rooms. It seemed that every time I went into a different room, I went into different countries. I thought that I would never get back home.

Then the man suddenly disappeared. I went back to the lookout tower and there it was, the treasure box that I had seen earlier. I was just about to grab it when the floor opened up and I slid down this slide into the moat.

Suddenly I woke up, soaking wet.

Lewis Brookbanks (11)
Orton Wistow Primary School, Peterborough

THE LADY WHO CAME FROM NOWHERE

On a gloomy Friday the 13th at around 2 o'clock, two girls, Fliss and Kenny, decided to go for a walk. Soon, it started to rain heavily. They sheltered underneath what looked like a porch at the front of a gloomy, forbidding-looking house.

'Kenny, what are you doing?' Fliss whimpered.
'Well, it's freezing out here, so I'm going inside to warm up,' Kenny protested.
'Are you mad? You don't know what's in there,' Fliss said.
Kenny ignored her and pulled the rusty bronze handle and stepped into the house, which was the size of a medieval castle.

Suddenly, a lady appeared from nowhere. Her crooked nose and bent chin were like the arrow on a compass facing north. Her hair was the colour of the flames in a forest fire . . . flaming red!

They stood as still as an ice statue. They tiptoed backwards, then they heard a bang. Fliss turned around, the door had slammed shut behind them. Fliss was shivering in fright. The lady walked towards them and they stepped back in shock. Kenny and Fliss ran to the door and pulled at the handle. Kenny pushed Fliss out of the way, she hit the handle with a metal pole. Suddenly the door opened, they ran out as quick as a flash.

The old woman ran out after them. They turned round, but in the blink of an eye, she was gone. A chilling wind flew past them as it said, 'Bye.'

Jasmine Ling (11)
Orton Wistow Primary School, Peterborough

THE GHOSTLY HOUSE

I woke up one morning and it was snowing, so I got dressed and went outside to play, but I heard a noise from the old house next door. But no one lived there, so I went to the house to see where the noise was coming from.

I knocked on the door. It was a very old door with a rusty postbox. I knocked on the door, but the door opened itself and the house was empty and there were creaky floorboards and spiderwebs everywhere. Then suddenly, the door banged shut. There were no lights, only an old-fashioned glass with a candle that had never been lit, so I looked to see if there were any matches. There were some matches under the table and only one had been used. So I lit the candle, that gave of a lot of light, so I had a walk around the house.

The noise came back. There was a ghost, I was sure there was. I screamed and ran outside and into my house. I shouted for my mum. I told my mum what had happened, but she didn't believe me. I kept on telling her. I never went in the old house ever again.

I always heard that noise but I didn't care and I still played out with my friends. Then a year passed, and the noise stopped. It never came back.

Jemma Keulen (11)
Orton Wistow Primary School, Peterborough

ONE NORMAL DAY FOR BOB UNDERWEIGHT

'We've got him now.'
It was the 5th of March and if you're wondering who I am, my name is Underweight, Bob Underweight, so sit back and listen to my story.

I was just having a normal drive in my Ferrari F50 when suddenly, Jasmine Porter and her servant Big Cat were chasing me.
'Hey, Big Cat, turn, turn,' Jasmine shouted as I turned the corner.
While Jasmine was being annoying, I was thinking of what to do next, when I crashed and put myself in more danger.

Quietly, Jasmine and Big Cat were on my trail, and the only thing to do was to pray.
'Over here, Jasmine,' I said.
'Big Cat stay here. I'll go alone.'

So she went and when she came, I kissed her. I don't know why I kissed her, but I did. After, she helped me kill Big Cat and we got married. That was a normal day for me, Bob Underweight.

Ben Brown (11)
Orton Wistow Primary School, Peterborough

THE CONCERT

It was Thursday and Kelly was up and dressed. She was excited because tonight, she was going to see the Beatles in concert.

At school, she was so busy thinking about that night that she was sent up to receive the cane, by strict Mr Batt. Wincing in pain, Kelly squeezed her hand, trying to reduce the burning feeling that was soaring through her body. Mind you, not all the money in the world could buy the exciting sensation of a Beatles concert!

It was the evening and Kelly was dressing up in her prettiest clothes and putting on her prettiest make-up, ready to meet the pop band of her dreams. At 7.30, Kelly left the house, looking gorgeous enough to make any boy's heart melt!

When they were there, the noise level inside the concert was deafening. And there, in the centre of the hall and standing on a podium, bellowing music and singing, were the glorious Beatles! Kelly loved them, their singing, their music, themselves and everything about them.

For two hours this brilliant concert went on and Kelly never lost her smiling face. Kelly was disappointed when it finished, but glowed red and blushed with embarrassment when John Lennon bent down and pecked her soft cheek with a kiss! Kelly was so happy, she said, 'This has been the best night ever!'

Krissie Dickens (11)
Orton Wistow Primary School, Peterborough

THE FIGHT

One morning at school, Alan and Chris were playing football and a beautiful girl walked through the school gates and Alan dropped the ball in amazement. He was stunned to see a girl like that. Alan and Chris ran as quickly as they could right to the tip of her toes. Chris and Alan said at the same time, 'Will you go out with me?'
'I don't know. I'll go out with the cutest. Alan, I'll go out with you,' said Fiona.
'I hate Alan,' said Chris.

Chris hit him round the head, and Alan got really mad and got up and hit him back. Chris started to get a nosebleed. All the teachers came out and told them to go to Mr Belding. They got really told off. Chris and Alan made up and they never spoke to the girl again.

James Harper (10)
Orton Wistow Primary School, Peterborough

IT

It was very late. The room was black and unusually quiet. Still Dan couldn't sleep. It was not that Dan wasn't tired, he was exhausted. He was afraid to go to sleep, in case 'It' came again. Dan couldn't be sure if It really had come, or if he had only dreamt it. Either way, Dan didn't want It to come again.

Before getting into bed, Dan had checked the windows and pulled the curtains. This was to prevent shadows. He didn't want any false alarms. He didn't want to be terrified, only to discover it had been a shadow. Imagine being terrified of your own shadow, or the shadow of a lampshade. What a wimp!

For two nights It had come. The awful smell, was it man or creature? It had a shape, yet wasn't solid, but it was strong, trying to drag Dan off his bed. It was silent as it moved. However, Dan felt is strength and heaviness when he tried to pull away. Dan had been so scared, he couldn't make a sound.

Finally Dan slept, only to be awoken by It, pulling at him. He froze. Perhaps if he went with it, It would leave him alone, but what if he couldn't get back? That might put him in more danger. Dan pushed at It, but still It came. The smell made him feel faint. Dan's heart was racing. He was lashing out with his arms and legs. Suddenly, Dan felt himself being lifted off the bed. It carried him away.

Owen Jones
St Mary Magdalene RC Combined School, Milton Keynes

MY SCREAM IS NOT HEARD

'Do you want to go up the park?' Emily asked, tucking a strand of her chocolate-brown hair behind her ear.
'OK,' replied Izzy, shutting her magazine.
The girls left the house and headed for the park. It was raining, so they brought their umbrellas along too, but the park had disappeared, vanished! Instead, there stood a large silver barrier blocking anything from view.
'What's happened?' exclaimed Emily, shaking with cold.
'I wonder what's inside that building?' Izzy wondered curiously.
'Oh please, don't wonder,' said Emily, now shaking with fear.
'I'm going inside,' Izzy decided aloud.

She opened the gate, then went inside. Right in front of her eyes was a tall, lanky building. Emily had disappeared, gone, leaving Izzy to cope by herself. Izzy could hear ringing staccato sounds, but nothing could get in the way of Izzy when she had set her mind to something. She kicked open the decrepit, rotting door with a sign saying: *Warning - dangerous,* but still Izzy carried on.

It smelt like a hospital corridor and looked like one too; it had a white floor, white walls and a white ceiling. It seemed like it had been forever to Izzy and her feet were aching badly, but still she carried on.

Finally she came to a door. She pushed it open to reveal three screaming children. Izzy started to run. She heard footsteps behind her, felt a hand on her shoulder, heard a scream; *her* scream, but was it heard?

Rachael Cunliffe (11)
St Mary Magdalene RC Combined School, Milton Keynes

RAYS OF LIGHT

It was Lucy's 12th birthday and she was running a birthday party at 4 o'clock, but all of her friends had turned up early.
'Happy birthday, Lucy!' Hannah said, handing over her present.

A few hours later, Lucy, Hannah and friends started to settle down, so they would be calm for when they went to sleep.
'Wow, look at the time!' Lucy said, amazed. 'We'd better go to sleep.'
'Nah,' Hannah replied, 'it's only 12.30.'
The girls started to settle down, but as they did so, they heard a noise coming from the backyard.
'What was that noise?' Hannah asked.
'How am I supposed to know?' replied Lucy in a high-pitched voice.
The girls had a discussion and decided that they should go and explore.

Once the girls reached the garden, they saw a ray of light.
'Let's follow it!' whispered Lucy.
In one straight line, the girls followed the ray of light to find themselves in the middle of an alley. There, stood in the middle of the alley, was an old man. He was tall, skinny and had long grey hair.
'Hello Lucy,' the man said.
'How do you know my name?' Lucy questioned.
'Because . . . I do!'
'You don't seem very sure.'
'No I'm not, darling! Faye, what are you doing out? Your mother will go spare . . . I'm not very good at lying am I?'
'No.'
The 'old man' removed his mask and turned out to be Lucy's father.
'Did I scare you?' Lucy's dad asked.
'Yes, at first!'
'Good!'

Alyssa Ash (11)
St Mary Magdalene RC Combined School, Milton Keynes

THE TRAGIC STORY OF AN ORPHAN

After experiencing tragic events in his live, seven-year-old Oliver had become a quiet and unhappy child. He'd been passed around different families, but no one would adopt him. After this, Oliver felt lost and heartbroken, he was like a worn out toy being tossed to and fro. He knew better now than to properly acquaint himself, get to like them, or he would be the one paying for it. No one knew how much it hurt. No one knew the effect it had on Oliver's happiness.

Oliver was packing his belongings into an old, battered suitcase. The hinges squeaked and it was covered in a mass of sellotape. At the sound of a loud, shrill voice, he carelessly shoved everything into his suitcase and ran swiftly down the chipped wooden stairs that creaked beneath his feet. Mary, a rather plump but serious woman with limp, lifeless, black hair, beckoned into the car and stood back to watch him leave.

Later, he arrived at a cottage with a variety of beautiful flowers.

After their success in getting Oliver to cooperate and do some errands, they found that he was a very sweet little boy.

Finally that day came and Oliver walked out to Mary and said gloomily, 'I'm ready.' A tear trickled down his face, it felt like a thousand daggers were piercing his heart.
'For what?' she sighed. 'They have adopted you.'
A sudden rush of warmth and relief washed over him.

From then on, he was known as Oliver Chant.

Tanya Frayne
St Mary Magdalene RC Combined School, Milton Keynes

CREEPY GOINGS ON!

Casey and Helga were jogging through the woods one day when all of a sudden, Casey screamed.
'What's wrong?' asked Helga.
'My ankle. Oh . . . I think it's sprained!' Casey panted, as it hurt so much she couldn't breathe.
'OK, right, hang on. Is this the third clearing?' enquired Helga.
'Yes, why? Ouch, my ankle!' replied Casey, clutching her ankle.
'Oh stop moaning,' snapped Helga. 'And it's 3.00, right?'
'Yeah,' replied Casey.
'Where's Josh? Maybe he's in that old manor, let's go and have a look,' said Helga, bending down to pick up her friend because she couldn't walk.
'I'm OK, it was just cramp,' giggled Casey.

As they entered, a voice moaned, 'Leave now.'
'Helga, I don't like this place; it's creepy,' whispered Casey timidly. But Helga had already started walking towards the stairs, so she reluctantly followed.
'How many more steps, Casey?' asked Helga.
'I don't know,' replied Casey.

Suddenly, on the last step, the floor gave way. They landed on a hard wooden floor.
'I told you, leave,' moaned the voice again.
'OK, I'm spooked,' shivered Helga.
'Me too,' agreed Casey, her face as white as a ghost. She was so frightened.
'Let's leave,' Helga began.
'No wait!' exclaimed a voice, a voice they knew.
'Josh!' they chorused.
'Sorry,' Josh began. 'Ha! So cheerleaders do get scared!'
'Yeah, and all footballers are scum,' finished Casey, flicking her long blonde hair.

Abigayle McCue (11)
St Mary Magdalene RC Combined School, Milton Keynes

CHILD OF WAR

I heard the air raid siren go off. It was quiet amongst the sound of bombs. We didn't panic. It had all been practised beforehand. Straight to the Anderson shelter. No wandering, no rescuing and certainly no turning back.

I was holding James's hand now. He was very young then and didn't clearly understand what was happening. It was when the stairs came into sight that I began to have doubts about my mother's and father's safety. The bomb sounded awfully close and I knew we were all in great peril.

I don't know what inspired me to turn back, but suddenly I was whispering to James to make his way to 'that secret hideout underground'. He was sobbing and looking like the average distraught four-year-old. I was rushing back the way I had come, moving towards my parents' bedroom. I couldn't see my parents, I was panic-stricken; and then they came into sight. Two dark figures holding onto each other in desperation. Smoking flames blurred my vision, my mama stifled a cry.

'Alice!' I heard my papa's croaky voice. 'Go!'
I simply couldn't leave them. Then I saw the flames spread across the room. All hope for my parents had suddenly vanished. Then strong hands gripped my shoulder. I turned and looked into the eyes of an army man. His pitying eyes confirmed my worst fears. I shuddered as a scream came from the bedroom; my mother's. I caught a glimpse of two dark figures lying amidst the flames, my parents. I never saw them again.

However, throughout my life, I can never stop picturing the final image of my parents lying together, surrounded by smoke and flames. It will haunt me for the rest of my life.

Nicki O'Hagan (11)
St Mary Magdalene RC Combined School, Milton Keynes

HAUNTED

Allow me to introduce myself. I'm Josephine and I have a sister called Lily.

Anyway, the story started last week when the phone rang. Little did we know, but some exciting news was on the end of it!
'I'm sorry, Mrs McAlly, but your dearest father has died this morning!'
'Thank you very much,' replied Mum, trying to sound sad. Mum put the phone down. Mum had never liked her father, he said that she was a mistake. 'Friday is the funeral, kids, and after, we'll have a party.'
'Yes!' we shouted excitedly.

After the funeral and the party, we started a streak of bad luck, like no other. First, our mum turned against us. She started hitting us and kicking as well. Then Dad. By the time they were finished, we were battered and bruised. The bookshelf fell on me and my sister got bullied today at school as well.
'What are we going to do?' I asked, curiously. Of course, Lily wasn't going to know the answer.

Our bad luck carried on, until yesterday, when I found out why our bad luck had repeated on us. I heard an evil laugh in Grandad's old bedroom, which he hadn't been in for ten years. I made my way up the stairs and along the decrepit hallway to the last door. I opened it quietly. It squeaked. I found the ghost of Grandad Geberdi, sitting on his bed, laughing his head off!

Claire Ennis (11)
St Mary Magdalene RC Combined School, Milton Keynes

RICHMOND AND SAMSON

Welcome to a day in the life of me . . . Samson Ferry.

'I'm rich! I'm rich!' I would call, every time my mother handed me a dollar. But that was then . . . this is now.

So here I am . . . the bum of 9th Street, New York. That dumb mayor comes round now and again, but he wouldn't notice a bum if one came up and smacked him. You see, the mayor, in all his glory, knows one thing and one thing only. He is rich and I am poor, and there is nothing I can do about it.

Welcome to a day in the life of Mayor Richmond Lynx.

'I'm rich! I'm rich!' I shout every time I slip down 9th Street. I don't feel like sharing my money; I don't think I ever will!

So here I am, the mayor of New York, minding the 'bums' of 9th Street and dining with the fellas down 1st Street. Hey! I'll let you in on a secret: I, the mayor, do the lottery every week. I don't see it as desperation, I see it as a test of my luck. Mind you, I wouldn't mind another bob or two.

It was Christmas Eve when the two did clash. Samson with a dollar note, Richmond with cash. Samson's numbers were so small, he could hardly win. He might as well have lobbed them in the bin! Richmond's numbers were more like it, they were big and small. His money would pile up so tall.

Kodjo Okutu (11)
St Mary Magdalene RC Combined School, Milton Keynes

THE KILLER SHADOW

Michael was walking home from school when some autumn leaves made a spiral in the air. Michael had seen something identical in a horror film, when people had got sucked into the wind and died. Michael started running away from it, his black hair and plump face bobbing up and down. On Michael's second step, he tripped over a twig, falling into another hole in the ground. 'Where am I?' Michael asked himself, when he landed on his chocolate bar.

Michael heard someone or something roar.
'Wh-wh-who said that?' Michael said, freaked out.
'Michael, I've been expecting you,' boomed a low voice.
Slowly and cautiously the small figure of Michael turned about, scanning his surroundings. Suddenly a tall, dark image slowly floated forward. Michael began to scram, but his throat quickly stopped it dead.
'Michael,' boomed a voice that seemed to come from every direction, 'come.'
The single word chilled Michael to the bone. Michael's body suddenly jerked forward without him wanting to. He felt drowsy.

Michael woke up in a dark room, his muscles frozen stiff. His eyes travelled to the shadow. Michael then noticed the curved blade in the shadow's hand. Michael drew his last breath, not realising. Michael lay there dead on the floor . . .

Adam Danielewicz
St Mary Magdalene RC Combined School, Milton Keynes

A Day In The Life Of John Parker

I, John Parker, have just arrived in Morocco with my father who has started his lectures. Morocco is an amazing place, it's like a giant sandcastle, as everything is made of sand.

I went to my dad's friend's house, who was called Mr Contal. 'Hello,' I smiled.
'Hello,' Mr Contal wheezed.
'What is the matter?' I wondered.
'There's a head in the market,' he said, looking horrified.

My parents were still out, so it seemed the perfect time. I got into disguise and snuck out of the house. I went to the market and asked if anyone knew where it was.
A man said, 'Follow me, I will show you.'
He led me into a clearing and . . .

I woke with my head pounding. I must have been knocked out. I seemed to be blindfolded and my hands and feet were tied up. I seemed to be on some animal, it was transporting me somewhere. Finally I arrived at a market, it seemed to belong to outlaws.

There were several other children there and some seemed to be younger than me, and I am only nine. A boy was put on the stage and the bidding began.
'50, 70, 100, 120 . . . *sold!*'
Then I was grabbed by the arm and pulled to the stage.
First, a white man said, '20,' then a new bidder said, '40.' The two men kept going, '60, 100.' It went on and on until, '500 . . . *sold!*'
I was taken, and the man shouted, 'Don't ever do that again!'
It was Mr Contal.

Antony Bailes (11)
St Mary Magdalene RC Combined School, Milton Keynes

The Ghost Train

Seventeen-year-old Nicky and her younger sister were strolling along the train station, searching for Platform 2. They were looking forward to seeing their dad. Two years ago, their parents had divorced and since then, their dad had been living in London.

Twelve-year-old Jessica (Nicky's sister) stared and pointed at the sign saying *Platform 2*. 'Come on, hurry up!'
The two sisters ran as they flicked their golden-blonde hair out of their faces, dragging their heavy suitcases behind them.
'Let's sit here,' Jessica announced in excitement, so they sat next to each other. Nicky pulled a magazine out of her bag and leaned it on her legs, while Jessica sat drawing.

'Whoo!' screamed Jessica as the train suddenly paused. They were stuck on a train in the middle of nowhere, in a dark and gloomy tunnel. Nicky was brave enough to stand up and go to the driver, but as she did so, she noticed there was no driver! She was just about to faint, but then she had an idea. She sat down in the driver's seat and grabbed hold of the controls. But then the lights started to flicker on and off. The scream of Jessica echoed, the roof began to vibrate.

Nicky snatched her cell phone, but as she did, everything stopped. Jessica sighed with relief as she wiped her tears off her face. Nicky hugged Jessica. While she was on the phone, she rang her dad up, but her dad wouldn't answer. All she heard was a scream!

Kelly-Ann Smith (11)
St Mary Magdalene RC Combined School, Milton Keynes

FREAKY

Sandy Bay was walking home from a tiring term at school. Overhead, she could see a nasty storm brewing. As it started raining, 'I forgot my raincoat,' grumbled Sandy, miserably shivering like she had seen a ghost.
As she walked further down the wet, murky road, she saw a rickety old manor. 'Ahhh, shelter at last,' she sighed in relief.

Inside the house, everything looked burnt and ancient. The roof had so many holes in it that the rain was seeping through.
'Hello there,' whispered a voice.
Sandy turned around and to her surprise, there was a girl standing in the doorway.
'My name is Helga,' said the girl politely.
'I'm Sandy,' she said timidly.
Helga looked pale and transparent, which made Sandy suspicious.

Sandy and Helga got to know each other and became good friends. Soon, Sandy trusted Helga, which was what Helga wanted. Sandy sat down on an old rug with Helga. 'I'll wait until the storm passes and then I'll leave.'
'I don't think so,' muttered Helga, with an evil grin on her face.
Helga left the room in silence. Sandy went looking for Helga, with the tension building.
'Say goodbye, my pretty!' screamed Helga, holding a butcher's knife.

With one swipe, Sandy was dead. Her blood raced out onto the floor and there she lay, dead. No one knows why Sandy was murdered. Maybe because Helga was a lonely ghost. But one thing is for sure, that was the last they ever saw of Sandy Bay.

Natasha Evans (11)
St Mary Magdalene RC Combined School, Milton Keynes

THE ATTIC

The middle of summer. The sun's glint blinding me. Even on this beautiful day I was bored. Nothing to do or see, nowhere to go. My skin started to crisp in the sun. I would be glad to take any offer to get out of here.

'Eric Ramsden, go upstairs and clean your room, now!' my mum screamed.

I was happy to take any offer, any offer but this. 'Coming Mum.'

I went exhaustedly up the stairs, step by step, until I reached the top. I was especially tired today. I could fall over any second now. But it didn't happen, as if destiny and fate were saying no. There was something I had to do. My empty, mindless brain dragged my legs forward. 'Ouch!' I groaned, and suddenly opened my eyes to see I had bumped into the airing cupboard door. I had never been in there. I went in. I wouldn't return.

It was very dark and spacious, so I walked in. I would have, if I hadn't tripped up on an open chest near the entrance. I got a torch and read, to my amazement, *To beloved Eric Ramsden, 1992 – 2003, June 13. RIP* on a gravestone!

I dropped the torch and fainted, never to be seen again. It took me.

This event took place on 13 June 2003.

Ramy Saad
St Mary Magdalene RC Combined School, Milton Keynes

DAVID THE DEMON HUNTER

At the end of school, David came across a woman. Her name was Teena and she wanted to meet David at the cemetery at 9 o'clock.
David said, 'Sure, but you'd better explain why.'
'I will,' said Teena.

That night, David eventually arrived 15 minutes late. David said, 'What did you want me here for?'
Teena just said, 'You are the one who will kill them all.'
David replied, 'Who are these things that I have to kill?' in a suspicious way.

Then all of a sudden, a weird creature appeared, with horns on its head and it had huge claws that looked like talons. It started slashing at David, but it kept on missing. Then David grabbed its arm and put it in an arm lock and broke its shoulder blade. Then the creature got scared and ran away.
'OK, what was that?' he said.
'It was a demon that you could have killed, but instead you scared it away.' Then Teena started explaining that David was a demon hunter.

David thought that she was crazy, but then Teena said, 'You bear the mark,' in a quiet voice.
David replied, 'What mark? What are you talking about?'
Teen said, 'The mark of the chosen ones.'
David thought for a moment. He said to himself, 'How did I scare that thing away? It must have been the mark!'

Teena vanished, leaving David with his thoughts. *How could this happen? Why me?* He headed home, feeling devastated.

Emlyn Northcote-Rojas
St Mary Magdalene RC Combined School, Milton Keynes

KILLER SKULL

'Charlie! Freddie! Come on, this way! Oh Charlie! Freddie! Stupid dogs!' Jess yelled across the giant field. They zoomed across the park field at fifty miles an hour. Just watching their little legs go mad made Jessie feel tired. She knew she couldn't keep up. After five minutes of running behind, she found them barking in a cave they had found behind a phone box.

'What's that? Something's glowing in the cave. Let's look,' whispered Jess.

The tunnel was at least ten minutes long. Suddenly, the dogs froze with their eyes wide open and hid behind Jessie's legs, growling. That's when they saw it - a coffin! A glowing coffin!

'What's happening? What's that noise?' screamed Jess.

There was banging, roaring, barking and suddenly . . . the coffin opened. There was silence. Jessie screamed when she saw what the rotting pile of bones held in its hand. A knife as long as a 30-centimetre ruler, covered in blood. The skeleton dived towards her aiming the knife at her throat.

'Freddie, no!' yelled Jess. Freddie jumped up in front of the skeleton, but got stabbed himself. Jess and Charlie ran out of the cave, not daring to look back.

'Quick Charlie, a phone box, I'll ring the police!' shouted Jess.

She bit her nails while she was waiting for someone to answer. Just then, she dropped the phone when she saw who was running towards her. 'Freddie!' she screamed. 'You're alive!' She bent down to hug him. 'I love you. You're the best dog ever, let's go to the park.'

Jess was so happy that she got Freddie back, until she found out what really happened with Freddie and the evil skeleton . . .

Abby Linehan (11)
St Mary Magdalene RC Combined School, Milton Keynes

THE GHOST WHO ASKS 'WHY?'

'Aahhh,' said a loud voice behind him.
Suddenly, Spook turned around to see his friend Sheets looking like a human (he had dressed up). *'Spook!'* he said loudly. 'You're supposed to *scare* me!'
'But why?' Spook asked in a confused voice.
'Because you're a ghost. Well you're meant to be, even if you're a disgrace to the ghosts' name.'

Spook turned sadly and started wailing as he walked through the wall to his room. Spook sat on his bed making his wailing sound and thinking about what had just happened. 'Why can't I scare people? Why can't I stop asking questions that start with why? Why am I scared of people?' he asked himself.

Later that day, Ghost (one of Spook's friends) came into Spook's room. 'We've decided that you have to go. I've found a haunted house for you to go to.'
'Why?' asked Spook.
'So you can practise your scaring skills.'

Spook walked down the winding path through the dark forest. He followed the path to a clearing and there was the haunted house!
'Hey, what are you doing here?' said a gloomy ghost behind him. 'Why don't you come inside?'

The next morning, Spook and the others all went outside into the forest where a family were having a picnic.
'Go on then,' said one of the ghosts. 'Go and scare them silly!'
Spook screamed and wailed around the family. Their baby started to cry, Spook felt sorry for them, so he started dancing instead.

'You're useless,' all the ghosts said, after Spook had several scaring lessons.
Spook wailed home to his bed and said, 'I'll have to get another job.'

Alison Carter (11)
St Mary Magdalene RC Combined School, Milton Keynes

NEVER TO BE SEEN AGAIN

Hi! My name is Jay Smith. I'm going to tell you a scary story. Ready?

It all happened when I was going for a day with my family to Thorpe Park. I needed the toilet, so I was on my way to the WC and I got lost. I had seen a pointy pit in the distance. I wasn't sure if I should go there or not, because part of my body said yes, go, and another part of my body said no, because it might be dangerous. So I had decided to go, when I went in the castle. I didn't need the WC anymore.

I opened the door and it slammed. There were cobwebs, broken doors, smashed windows and dust everywhere. So then two or three hours had passed. I was getting tired. Another four hours had passed and I heard someone cry, louder and louder each time.
'Who's there?' I shouted. No answer, so I shouted out the second time and a reply came from the library. It was a girl. I asked her name and she cried,
'Joelle, I'm 13 years old.'
She told me her story and that she got lost in the storm. Same as me.

We were hungry, but there was nothing to eat at all.
'I'm hungry,' moaned Joelle, so did I.
Then I got a chill in my back. I was cold. The temperature dropped so much that we huddled together to keep warm, but unfortunately, we were found two days later by a park assistant, frozen to death in each other's arms.

Angela Mulé (11)
St Mary Magdalene RC Combined School, Milton Keynes

The Candle

Melanie and Rachel were best friends. They went to a fête held in their town that was selling exotic goods from around the world. They saw a tent made from Arabian carpets. Outside the tent, a sign said *Mystic Goods Sold Here*.
'Shall we go in?' said Rachel.
'Yes,' answered Melanie.
They saw lots of weird things, however, one thing caught their eye.
'Look at that candle, it's lovely. Let's get it.'
'OK,' said Rachel.
They bought it, when suddenly an old man mysteriously appeared, who said, 'Do not light that candle.'

Later on that day, curiosity got the better of them and they lit the candle. Without warning they were transported back in time.
'Where are we?' said Rachel.
'The Stone Age,' said Melanie.
'You mean dinosaurs, that kind of thing?' replied Rachel.
They heard the *boom, boom* of dinosaur feet, and were frightened. They ran for shelter in a cave.

'I think the only way home is to light the candle again,' said Melanie.
'But we need matches,' said Rachel.
They heard a rustling in the cave and there behind them was a *cave girl*.
'Matches . . . matches . . .' said Rachel.
'She won't understand you, you need to say fire . . . fire . . .'
The cave girl handed Rachel two sticks.
'What am I supposed to do with these?' she said.
The cave girl snatched them back, rubbed them together, sparks came off and one stick caught fire. The dinosaurs were outside the cave. Rachel quickly lit the candle and waved goodbye to the cave girl. They were transported back to their home, safe and sound.

They decided never to light the candle again. *Well, possibly!*

Emily Farrier (11)
St Mary Magdalene RC Combined School, Milton Keynes

THEY'RE FAKE

'Suzy, where did you put that big brown box we had delivered today?' asked Anne.
'I have already put it on the shelf,' replied Suzy.
'Oh, right. What was in it anyway?'
'Toy guns,' said Suzy, opening and shutting the till.

After a little while, a man came into the shop and bought a toy gun. Then after another little while, a man came in and bought a toy gun, and another.

That night when Suzy and Anne were counting the money out of the till, they spoke about the day.
'Well, those toy guns sold very well,' said Anne, looking at all the money on the table.
'I think we should take it down to the bank right away,' Suzy told Anne.

They walked to the bank and when they got there, there were loads of men with guns in their hands.
'Open the safe now!' shouted one of the men.
'Aahhh!' screamed the till lady.
'Don't bother,' Anne told the lady. 'Don't be afraid. Suzy, don't those guns look exactly the same as the ones we were selling in the shop?'
'Oh yes, definitely,' Suzy said, quickly snatching one out of a man's hand. 'They are. Look it says 'made in China, toy guns'.'
At that point, the police ran in and arrested them.
'Who phoned the police?' groaned one of the men.
'I did,' said the bank manager, holding a phone in his hand.

Anne and Suzy were rewarded for their bravery by the bank manager, and even ended up in the local newspaper.

Sarah McGlynn (11)
St Mary Magdalene RC Combined School, Milton Keynes

KATE'S SPOOK

Kate was in Year 3 and she'd been bullied since Reception. Kate had long black hair that always shimmered in the sun. Everybody said that Kate was teacher's pet. Not only that, they punched and kicked her for being smart and pretty.
Until one day, the bullies said, 'If you want us to stop bullying you, then go down Spook Street and go through the scary passage door.'
Because she wanted to stop being bullied, she said yes.

That night, she started to walk down terrible Spook Street. She walked for ages and finally got to the passageway. She followed the pathway. She hurried down the passageway and the front doors shut . . .

She turned around, the doors weren't open. She ran and banged on the doors; nothing happened. She said to herself, 'This is like what the spooky story said. Whoever goes in, never comes out!' Her pretty, pale blue eyes widened in fright. The words ran through her head until she couldn't stand it anymore, so she screamed.
Suddenly, Kate heard voices, ghostly voices saying, 'Find two doors. Go through one of them to your death, and one of them will bring you safely back home.'
The doors appeared and so she chose left, because she wrote with her left hand. Was she right? Kate walked in, she started swirling. She felt like one thousand hands were slapping her.

The next morning, she woke up with a thumping headache. She wondered, was it all a dream?

Nicole Hawes (11)
St Mary Magdalene RC Combined School, Milton Keynes

TIME

Josh was an ordinary school boy, but nothing ordinary happened to him from the day he became a science lover.

It was lunchtime in school and Josh had not realised that in that same hour, he would have to fight for his life.
'Josh! Come on, we'll be late! Hurry!' shouted Tara, Josh's best friend. Josh ran after her. They were going to test the time machine Josh had made, to see the future. When they arrived at their science room, they pulled open the door of the machine and stepped inside. With the pull of a lever, they were zooming through time. *Whoosh!*
'Now, I wonder where we landed?' said Tara excitedly as she opened the door again.

Around the two explorers were hundreds of *aliens!* Each one with its own look.
'Um . . . Tara . . . I think we should get out of here!' exclaimed Josh.
They turned round, and to their surprise, the time machine was further away than it had been a minute ago. They were chased towards it by the aliens, and when they reached it they jumped in, pulled the lever and were sent back to school, just in time for science class.
'Right, now class,' said Miss Tay, 'what do you think is going to happen in the future?'
Both Josh and Tara put their hands up.
'Aliens will take over the planet,' said Tara when she was asked.
'Yeah, and they will hate all humans,' finished Josh.

Jade Kavaliauskas (11)
Thomas Eaton Primary School, Wimblington

GRANDFATHER'S SPECIAL TROUSERS

One bright, sunny morning, Tim the shopkeeper felt very weird. He was wearing trousers which his grandfather had given him before he had passed away. This was the first time Tim had worn the trousers since his grandfather had passed away.

Tim started to do his work and he was very happy and joyful while he was doing his work. Tim was never as happy and joyful in his life. Tim never liked working, but since he wore the trousers, he loved work.

When it was time for Tim's break, he went to hang around with his friend Sam. Sam was always happy and an exciting boy, but Tim usually hung around on his own, so this was a surprise for Sam. Tim and Sam went to buy a sandwich. When Tim got his money bag out, he found a note which said, 'To my grandson Tim, these trousers are very special, they make you have a happy, joyful and exciting day, *so please look after them.*'

Now and again, Tim wore his grandfather's trousers so he could have a good time and a good laugh. When Tim did not have his grandfather's trousers on, he felt a bit different. He felt very lonely and sad.

When Tim was grown up, he got married and had a child called Tom. Tom was the name of Tim's grandfather. Tom was a boring boy, so boring no one wanted to be friends and no one wanted to play with him. When Tim was 70, he decided that he would give the special trousers to Tom, because he knew Tom was very sad because he had no friends.

When Tom wore the trousers, he was very happy and he had so many friends. Tom loved the trousers so he looked after them and gave them to his son.

Tahmina Begum (11)
William Austin Junior School, Luton

THE TALES OF MELDORE

Our tale begins long ago on the shores of Meldore, in the sacred land of Domrock, where the powerful wizard Zingard lived. He was leader of the Norlay people who lived in undisturbed lands. For many years they ran wild on the moors. However, Zingard was not there very often; he was searching the forgotten corners of the land for the great ice castle that kept peace in the world. Ever since it was lost, darkness had begun to creep over Meldore. Zingard's brother was consumed by this evil and travelled to Hefnom where many other dark creatures hid and gained power.

'Master, we are ready to destroy all the peace that is left in this world.'
'Excellent . . . take your minions. Make every worthless creature fall to the wrath of Lord Quadzink.'

His minions did not know pain or love, they did not eat or sleep, they travelled day and night. Zingard's world began to crumble, his peaceful cities fell into the darkness; if he didn't stop it, the whole of Meldore would soon be engulfed too.

Hours after taking Domrock, Zingard was surrounded by evil minions, who swiftly hopped aside for Holnok to confront him.
'You will perish!'
'You can fight this, don't give in, remember all the good times!'
'Yes, brother, let's show them who's boss!'
'*Never!*' boomed Lord Quadzink. '*Ondukus!*'
Holnok fell to the ground.
'You will leave this land forever! *Hondalakartus!*'
But he knew the battle was far from over.

Marcus Doyle (11)
William Austin Junior School, Luton

WHAT IS THE STORY?

The media is full of it, in newspapers, radio and television. The headlines are 'War Has Begun In The East'. In Okar, one man, Nutty Roam, is responsible. He has ruled for decades, bringing fear and poverty to his people. Western nations have sent in troops to bring down the reign of terror on these people and free them to live in harmony.

The ground forces are merging inland from all sides. On the southern side of Okar, the land is derelict, with no sign of life, just caves. The soldiers in their line of duty have made an amazing discovery, deep in the caves. They have found a small child, alive, dressed in what looks like sheets made of gold. He does not speak any language, but has led them to what seems like another world, with ancient buildings symbolising temples of stone, some plated in gold and precious stones. Most buildings are still intact as they seem to be very deep underneath the caves. There is no sign of any other life there and there is no history of any underworld record. Amazingly, who is this little boy? The soldiers have doubled their work; they are now not only fighting the war, but also guarding a precious world which hopefully will bring riches to its people, to build a better and prosperous future. The mystery of the boy still remains. What is the story?

Aksa Ahmed (11)
William Austin Junior School, Luton

A Day In The Life Of My Pet Dog, Bruiser

I've got a pet dog called Bruiser, he's a boxer. He is *so* cute! He has a very short tail and big, sad eyes, plus an adorable, squashed face. He will be ten years old on 24th June 2003 (that's seventy in dog years).

Bruiser never sleeps! My mum's alarm goes off at 6.45, but Bruiser makes sure she's awake. Then he has his morning walk. My mum drags herself out of bed and puts her clothes on. (I'm not supposed to tell you this, but she puts them on top of her pyjamas!) Bruiser walks my mum. (Whoops! I mean my mum walks Bruiser.) He drags her around the field. When she gets home, she does *most* of the jobs that need doing.

My dad (Andrew) gets up and sets off to work in Milton Keynes at 7.30. I get ready for school and walk up the road with my mum. Then she goes to work in London.

Meanwhile, Bruiser mopes around doing nothing, poor thing! Although throughout the day he's bound to be up to something mischievous, like chewing a shoe! When my dad gets home from work at 6.00, he feeds Bruiser his dinner, eg, fish, chicken, rabbit etc. We pick up my mum and then my dad walks Bruiser. After that, Bruiser cuddles up to us and snuggles down to sleep, ready for his un-busy day tomorrow!

Chloe Organ (8)
William Austin Junior School, Luton

A Day In The Life Of A Cat

I woke up early, stretched and yawned, then I crept downstairs to my food bowl. *Oh no, empty again,* I thought. I went back upstairs to wake my master. 'Come on, it's time to feed me,' I miaowed.

After I got fed and licked my lips, I went outside to find a nice warm spot in the garden to sleep. I was woken suddenly by a bird in the tree, but I was not bothered to chase it and went back to sleep.

I woke up and felt like going on an adventure, so I climbed over the fence into the next garden. I was hiding in the long grass when I heard a bark. It was a dog, it was getting closer. When it was nearly on top of me, I had to jump over the fence. I ran through my cat flap and decided to have some more food.

When I went to my bowl it was empty, so I went to my master and he came and fed me. As he opened the can, I thought to myself, *I hope it's tuna,* licking my lips.

Now my tummy was full, I went upstairs for a snooze. When I woke up it was morning. It was a new day for a new adventure and yes, my plate was empty again.

Alice Trotter (11)
William Austin Junior School, Luton

A Ghost Story

It was twilight, I was alone in my bedroom. My mum and dad were at the hospital, my brother was at Cubs. My curtains looked like shadowy, gloomy monsters. I immediately dived under the duvet. I was terrified. The door banged. Slowly I closed my eyes, what was I going to do? I heard a floorboard creak. What was it? Who was it? The curtains billowed out. My knees were shaking. The window rattled. I saw a twinkle at my door, it looked like a key. My lamp fell on the floor. I turned over in a tremble. How was I supposed to get to sleep?

I heard faint footsteps coming closer and closer. I grabbed hold of my teddy. I thought it was the end, then the door handle turned, slowly as a star. The door opened. It was my mum and my brother.
'My golly Moses, what is that? A torch? Switch it off. We have just come up to see if you were asleep. What's the matter? Are you scared?'
'No. Do you think I was? Anyway, you sounded like an elephant coming up those stairs. My lamp has fallen on the floor.'
'Don't cry over that.'
'Do you really think I was going to?'

Siân McIsaac (8)
Woodnewton Junior School, Corby

A Ghost Story

I was walking down a cold and quiet street. Nothing moved. I was a bit scared. I was going to my granny's. My big brother did not want to come. It was very cold because it was dark. It started to rain. Oh dear, I got wet.

I ran round a corner and I slipped on a puddle. Ouch! I got up. Just as I was getting up, I heard a noise, what was it? Who was it? The dry leaves crunched. Someone was walking on them. A branch snapped, I watched it fall. *Splash!* The branch landed in a puddle.

Someone was on their bike. They rang the bell on the bike. Why would they? I saw a shadow. That person rang the bell again. Now I was really scared. Someone called my name. I did not dare to speak. The wind rustled. I heard the bell again. 'Hello,' I said.
'Hello,' someone said.

They were coming closer. I jumped. *Crash!* I heard someone cry. I turned around. I took five footsteps back. The crying stopped. I ran behind a tree. I saw my brother's bike.
'Boo!'
'Argh!'
My brother made me jump. 'Come on, I'll take you to Gran's. Were you scared?'
'Yes, you made me jump!'

Savannah Cook (8)
Woodnewton Junior School, Corby

A Ghost Story

It was twilight, I was alone in the house. Everything was still and silent. The fridge looked like a tall giant.

As it turned midnight, I started to feel a bit scared. Suddenly, I heard a floorboard creak. Who was it? I was in the kitchen, so I went to see what it was.

I went upstairs and turned on the lights, I saw nothing. So I went downstairs and turned on the light in the living room. I heard a faint rustle. I was thinking that something fishy was going on. I ignored it. It happened again. My blood went cold. What was it? I went to see what it was, but nothing was there. I went back inside. I heard a breeze.

I heard a knock at the door. I answered it. There was no one there. I came out and I walked along the path. I couldn't see or hear anything. I walked a bit faster until I came to a big hedge. I stopped, I heard a funny noise in the hedge. I looked in it, there was nothing there. So I carried on walking. I came to a noisier hedge. I looked in there and it was my cat. I took it back home and gave it a wash.

Zoë Johnson (8)
Woodnewton Junior School, Corby

A Ghost Story

I was in the wood. It was just about twilight. I was drawing a picture of the trees, I had just finished. I went on to flowers, all I could hear was my pencil.

When I had finished, I was going on a stroll. All was silent, all was still. I thought I heard a footstep, I thought it was all in my imagination. I continued to walk.

Ten minutes later, I heard it again. I turned around, I thought I saw a shadow flitter between the trees. I started to run as fast as possible, but my legs could not carry me that fast. I looked back as I was running. I could not see the shadow anymore. I began to slow down, I got slower as the minutes went on, then I started to walk. I sat down because I was gasping for breath, but then I saw a shadow again. I wanted to get up and run, but my legs would not let me, they had fallen asleep.

What was that shadow? I don't know. The footsteps were coming closer and closer. It was my brother after all.
He said, 'I am coming to take you home! I was just messing about.'
But I think there was something sinister in the wood.

Sophie McShane (8)
Woodnewton Junior School, Corby

A GHOST STORY

I was in the cloakroom trying to find my homework, but I couldn't find it. Then I realised that I was looking in the wrong cloakroom, so then I went into the other cloakroom. I looked under the benches and heard some soft footsteps coming. It felt like they were right behind me. I looked slowly behind me, but nobody was there, so I carried on trying to find my homework. I thought to myself, *who was it?*

I could have left it in my drawer in the classroom. I looked in my drawer, but it wasn't there. Then I froze, because I thought someone was behind me, but no one was there. Then I heard footsteps coming my way. I got really scared. Someone touched my shoulder. It was my brother. He said, 'What is taking you so long to find your homework?'
I said, 'Because I can't find it.'
My brother said, 'Have you looked in your bag?'
'No,' I said.
'Well look in it.'
So I looked in it and there it was. So we went home, but not through the forest.

Shannen Garfitt (8)
Woodnewton Junior School, Corby

A Ghost Story

I was in the really big house. My mum and dad were out. My brother was in bed. It was dusk. I heard my brother snoring. All was still, all was quiet.

Suddenly *creak*. What was that? Who was that? I was frightened. I froze. I heard soft footsteps coming closer and closer, *pad, pad, pad*. I looked out of the living room door, but there was nobody there. Then I heard them again. I heard the front door open. I looked out of the window, I saw two shadows coming. I trembled all over. The handle turned slowly, I hid behind a chair and watched the door begin to open. It was Mum and Dad.
'Why are you hiding?'
'I was just playing around.'

Opal Gilchrist (8)
Woodnewton Junior School, Corby

A Ghost Story

It was night. I was alone in my bedroom. My brother slept downstairs. All was still, all was silent. I covered my head with the duvet and I fell asleep. Then I woke up and I took the duvet off my head. I was reading 'Goosebumps' till 9 o'clock. Suddenly the curtains billowed, I was frightened. Then I heard the floorboard creak. I jumped under my bed, but I was scared. I took the cover off my head and they stopped. They came back on again, I froze. I shouted out, nobody answered back. I could hear footsteps, they were coming closer. My lamp went on and off. I was afraid.

A door banged. I heard someone sweeping up in the kitchen. I was terrified. I heard footsteps coming upstairs, something moving. I thought this was the end. My light switched on, nails stuck into my head, the nails got taken out of my head. Ouch, that hurt. I fell over something, I hurt my stomach. I took the duvet off my head. It was my brother, do you think I was playing around?

Callum Raine (8)
Woodnewton Junior School, Corby

GHOST STORY

It was twilight, my mum was at hospital. My brother was sleeping downstairs. I was all alone upstairs, under my quilt. I was scared. Suddenly I heard the curtains billow. There was a *creak*, I heard footsteps coming up the stairs, slowly, slowly. *Bang!* I was scared because it was my first time looking after someone. Then I heard a *crunch!* on my bedroom door. I was scared to pen it. The handle came down, I hid under my duvet. The door opened, someone yawned. Someone or something was walking, then something sat on my bed. I slowly, slowly took the quilt off. It was my dog. *Woof! Woof!*

Curtis Dennison (8)
Woodnewton Junior School, Corby

A Ghost Story

It was dusk. I was in the woods. All was silent and still. I had just finished sketching the flowers in the woods. I read 'Goosebumps' for an hour. I started reading at 9 o'clock. I sketched some birds.

I saw a glowing eye, what was it? Was it a wolf? I ran faster and faster. I was gasping for breath, so I stopped. I heard a bark, a loud bark. I thought that it was going to be the end. I screamed. I fainted on a thorn. 'Ouch!' I said.

I got up and ran as fast as I could. I heard a howl, a twig snapped. I jumped. It was coming closer, because I could hear its footsteps on the leaves, *crunch, crunch!* I fainted. I heard my dad's voice.
He said, 'I am coming to take you home, with Mathrick, our dog. Why were you running away?'
Mathrick licked me in the face. I said, 'OK.'
We walked to the tent, the big tent. I fell asleep at 12 o'clock.

James Beattie (8)
Woodnewton Junior School, Corby

GHOST STORY

One foggy evening when it was dark, I was walking down the long street coming home from cubs. All was quiet. All was still. I was running quickly because it was 10 o'clock. I felt unsafe because I had no grown-ups with me. Suddenly, a tree swayed from side to side. I said to myself, 'It must have been the wind.'

Owls started hooting suddenly. A shadow flitted across me. I heard soft, padding noises. Suddenly a shadow flitted between the trees again, but just then, again I heard footsteps coming closer, closer and closer! I screamed as a loaded machine gun. I ran faster and faster. Suddenly I tripped. I thought this was the end for me.

I heard my brother's voice. 'I came to pick you up.'

Do you think it was? After all that, my brother said he was walking in the other direction. I was more scared then.

Andrew Payne (8)
Woodnewton Junior School, Corby

A Ghost Story

I was in the school, I had left my bag there. I quickly ran back to get it. When I got there, the doors were open. All the teachers were gone. I saw the caretaker picking litter up. All was silent. All was still. All was quiet.

I heard a noise coming from the classroom and I went to see what it was. I froze. I saw something move under the table. I quietly ran out, the caretaker was gone. I looked everywhere. I couldn't find him anywhere.

It wasn't a monster, it was the caretaker cleaning litter under the table, and the cleaner was doing it as well. It was just the cleaner and the caretaker.

Mark Taylor (8)
Woodnewton Junior School, Corby

A Ghost Story

It was in the middle of the night. I went home and left my book bag. I went back, no one was there, but there was only one man picking litter up. I crept in to get it. I went to the cloakroom. All was still. All was silent. All was quiet. I saw a shadow. I looked back, it jumped to the side.

I was in the classroom now to get it. I went to my drawer, it was not there. I heard footsteps at the door. I looked, I called out. No answer. What was it? Who was it? The door handle slowly turned. My heart was beating fast, my knees trembled. I closed my eyes. The door opened. I turned around. I heard my mum's and my brother's voices and they said,
'Why are you hiding?'
'I was just playing around.'

Do you think I was?

Daniel Murray (8)
Woodnewton Junior School, Corby

CAMPING IN THE WOODS

A bee was dancing in the hot, bright sun. Michael and Graham were watching the yellow daffodils dance in the sun.

'Why don't we put up the tent now?' said Graham.

By dusk, Michael and Graham had set up camp. It was getting late, very late. The sky was looking gloomier and gloomier and it was feeling chilly. A misty fog came nearer, nearer to the campsite.

'I'm frozen,' moaned Graham, 'I'm going to get some firewood. You stay here and look out for strangers.'

Michael heard something snap. 'What was that?' Graham had just gone, so it couldn't be him. There it was again. Michael felt a shiver race down his spine. Carefully he peered round the edge of a dark tree. A shadow shot quickly as an arrow. His heart was beating fast. Could it be a squirrel? No, squirrels don't come out at night. Michael peered round a little more.

'Boo! Got ya!' It was only Graham.

Alice Dunn (8)
Woodnewton Junior School, Corby

CAMPING IN THE WOOD

Graham and Michael were forced into the small tent.
'You go and get some firewood for the fire.'

By dusk, Michael and Graham had set up their tent. It was big, very big. The wind was howling through the whistling trees.
'I'm freezing,' moaned Graham. 'I'm going to get some firewood. You stay here and stay guard.'

When Graham had gone, Michael started to peel some carrots next to the tent with a bucket of water. Michael started to feel a cold shiver across his back. Soon, he went in the dark wood, his feet crushing leaves on the black ground below him. He heard a noise. He peered round the tree.
'Boo! Got ya! Ha, ha!' It was only Graham, returning back with wood.

Clark Usher (8)
Woodnewton Junior School, Corby

THE DARK WOODS

The wind blew harder and harder. Michael fell in a muddy puddle because of the heavy rucksack.
'Let's put the tent up,' said Graham.

By dusk, Michael and Graham had set the tent up. The chilly wind swooped in and out of the gloomy trees.
'I am freezing!' shouted Graham.

When Graham had gone to get firewood, Michael started to clear the ground. Suddenly, a leaf crunched. Michael froze. What was that? It couldn't be the wind, because it had died down. Michael's stomached chinged like cymbals, *ching, ching*. Michael crept in and out of the dark trees. What was that? Was it an eagle? No, because eagles are in Africa. Michael's face went as white as a ghost.
'Boo!' Graham laughed!

Ryan McKimm (7)
Woodnewton Junior School, Corby

SUSPENSE SUNDAY

It as a damp, cold night. Peter's mum and dad were shopping. He scuffled to his friend's house.

Peter brought Lee to his house. Peter called Lee, but he didn't answer. He called him again. 'Phew!' He answered. Lee saw a shadow. Who or what was that? He ran to the other window.
'Oh! It is just a black dog!' Lee sighed with relief, and the dog scuffled away. Just at that moment, Peter felt a hand . . . but still he didn't know what was tapping his shoulder. It felt sharp, like the claws of a tiger. Cautiously he went to turn. He grabbed what was touching him. It was . . . the branch of a tree poking through the window. Phew!

As they started to move, there was a *crash!* They were so scared, they wanted to get away. Lee's heart was racing as fast as a hare. Peter ran with Lee to his house. Lee's and Peter's hearts were racing. A minute later they heard a car. Lee and Peter went over to Peter's house.
'Mum! Mum! Where are you?' Peter said.
'Here,' Peter's mum said.
Peter ran upstairs, he heard a *woof, woof!* Phew! It was Peter's dog.
'I wonder what the screaming noise could have been?'

Liam Jackson (7)
Woodnewton Junior School, Corby

ANNANCER AND HER DREADFUL DAY

All alone Annancer was in her house. The house was a type of Indian house, with hay on the roof and metal to keep the house up. Annancer's mum and dad had gone to Africa to get some water from the well.

Annancer heard some footsteps outside, they were getting nearer and nearer. Annancer started to shake. The footsteps stopped. Annancer heard banging outside. She gasped. Annancer remembered it was the Indians playing the drums. Annancer saw a man coming towards her house. The man got nearer and nearer. The man's shadow got closer and closer. Annancer looked outside. It was her dad telling her that her mum went to see her sister and she would be back soon.

An hour later, she came back, and it was back to normal.

Tayla Marshall (8)
Woodnewton Junior School, Corby

IN THE SHED ALONE

All alone, Simon was in his shed collecting his Yu Gi Oh! cards. The shed had a spider's web hanging from the window. Simon was wearing the new England kit. *It is very dark,* he thought. 'Let's go then,' he whispered.

A tap on the windowpane. The spider's web went flying off. Simon froze. *Gasp!* Simon sprinted. Simon saw a shadow. *Huh!* Simon heard a bark. 'Oh, it's just my Staff,' wailed Simon.

Simon heard a big, loud scream. Something touched him.

Suddenly, he tripped over a step. Thankfully, Simon saw his brother. 'Mum wants you in, Simon.'

Simon walked to Mum. Simon's brother followed him in. He was relieved to have his family with him again, now he was safe.

Llwyd Campbell (7)
Woodnewton Junior School, Corby

THE DARK, CHILLY NIGHT

It was a dark, chilly night and Louise was sitting in her bedroom. She was reading Harry Potter, while her mum and dad were sleeping. She got up to chapter 5, so she went back into bed to see if she could get to sleep. She tried to get back to sleep for an hour. She got hot, so she went to carry on reading Harry Potter. Then she got bored with reading Harry Potter.

Louise sat on her bed, she was thinking what to do. She found her book under the cover. She picked it up and started to read it and then she heard a noise. It was like a witch noise. Her heart was beating like a drum and her tummy felt funny. She turned her head and Louise froze for five seconds and said to herself, 'It can't be Mum because she is sleeping, and so is Dad. It's just an old lady taking her dog for a walk.'

Louise looked out of her window and it wasn't the lady taking the dog for a walk, because Louise didn't see anybody. Louise went to tell her mum and dad, but they were fast asleep, and she was wrong. It was her mum and dad snoring. Her mum and dad woke up. Her mum saw Louise's frightened face, she wanted to find out what was wrong. Louise explained about the creepy, chilling sounds.
Mum just laughed and said, 'Go to bed!'

Rachael McAllister (8)
Woodnewton Junior School, Corby

THE SHADOW

Lara was in her bedroom watching TV. Mum and Dad had to go to the shops. She didn't want to go.

She went to get something to eat. She heard a bang at the door. So Lara opened the door . . . but no one was there. The gate opened, a roar, quickly Gran came and yawned. It was like a roar. Then Mum and Dad came home.

Lara went upstairs. She saw a shadow. Lara followed the shadow. The shadow went in her mum's bedroom. She looked in her mum's bedroom. When she looked, the shadow wasn't there. She went back downstairs.

So Lara told her mum about the shadow, then Lara went to bed.

Hayley Skinner (7)
Woodnewton Junior School, Corby

MUSEUM AT MIDNIGHT

Buzz, buzz, buzz, slam!
'What happened?' said Danny as he looked at Carl's blue eyes, so wide his eyeballs nearly fell out.
Hoot! Roar! Stamp!
Carl shivered, then sulked. 'Danny, what is it?' he squealed.
Danny turned his dusty face and came face to face with an electronic T-rex! The two boys sprinted, the dinosaur smashed everything in its path, including the award for being best museum trophy.
'Ter, run, he, saw, us,' said Danny.
'We lost him,' said Carl, gasping for breath.
Smash!
Danny looked at Carl and whispered, 'What happened?'
Carl looked at the shattered piece of glass. 'Does that answer your question?'
Rrroooaaarrr! Aaahhhhh!

They ran for their lives, followed by their uninvited visitor, going through many corridors.
Danny asked, 'First a dinosaur, what next?'
'Oh no, a dead end!' shouted Carl.
The T-rex closed in on them.
'This is the end!' screamed Danny. 'Duck!' he yelled.
'Where?' asked Carl. 'Oh!'
He ducked underneath the dinosaur.
Rooaar!
'Hey, what does this button do?' Carl asked himself as he pushed the button.
Creeaak! Boom! The dinosaur made an opening in the wall.
'Good Dino, now we'll forgive you if you stop saying '*roar*', OK?' said Danny cheekily.
Ne-nor, ne-nor.
'My knee's sore!' shouted Carl.
'We'd better take you home,' exclaimed a policeman.

Jack Barwell (8)
Woodnewton Junior School, Corby

THE FRIGHTENING DAY

Todd was walking home by himself on a warm spring day. He was walking down the street. There was a big grey bin at the end of the street. Todd heard sloppy footsteps. 'Who's that?' he wondered. The footsteps were coming closer and closer. 'Who's there?' Todd shouted. 'Just an old lady, *phew!*' he said.

Todd heard something scratching. Todd gasped, only a tiny little mouse. Todd felt something cold in the big grey bin. *What could it be?* He though in his mind. So Todd quickly opened the bin and looked inside, before anyone could see. It was a drinking can. Todd started running to his house. Just then, Todd's mum pulled up in her shiny silver car. Before Todd knew it, he was up in bed, snoring away. He never heard sloppy footsteps or scratching, and he never felt cold things ever again.

Siân Davis (8)
Woodnewton Junior School, Corby

Sarah And The Shadow

All in the dark, Sarah sat up in her bedroom alone, reading. Suddenly, a strange noise and shadow appeared from around the corner. Who or what was it? Sarah peered around the bedroom door. Sarah quickly looked back, she still could not see who or what it was. Sarah heard the noise again. *Tweet! Tweet!* Someone came home, who was that? Sarah worried. She tried to ignore the strange noise, but it came nearer. Sarah got scared. She hid inside the closet. In came a bird.

A bird! A big fuss over a bird! Phew.

Rebecca Curtin (8)
Woodnewton Junior School, Corby

HOME ALONE

All alone, Tony sat in his bedroom. It was a cold winter's night. Tony's mum went to Asda to do a bit of shopping. Watching TV, after a little while Tony got scared because the TV turned off and it was silent. Then Tony heard a *creaky, creaky* noise. Tony was scared.

It was very, very dark. He didn't know what to do. He felt something sharp and he screamed. What could it be? His heart was pounding, his legs would not move. He took a deep breath and turned. Oh, it was only his mum back from Asda.
'Sorry, Tony, I didn't scare you did I?'

Melissa Vaghela (8)
Woodnewton Junior School, Corby

THE WALK OF TERROR

Tim was strolling down the corridor and he heard a very strange noise. It was like this: *squeak, squeak.* Quickly, he rushed over to the sofa and hid behind it. his heart was thumping, he was horrified. What shall I do? He clenched the sofa and pulled himself up. Next, he went into the kitchen. *Argh! He heard that noise again.* 'Who, or what was it?' he said, terrified.

Meanwhile, Tim went upstairs, *trip, trip, trip, trip.* Finally he reached the top. *Argh!* That noise again, but this time it came closer and closer.
'Ouch!' he said. 'It was only a noise. Wait a minute, it must have been that squeaking noise.'
Later on, Tim thought he heard the strange, familiar noise. *Ching!* It sounded like it was the frying pan, maybe it was. So Tim went slowly into the kitchen. He saw a shadow and heard the echo of footsteps. He cautiously followed the footsteps.

Argh! Argh! It was only the wind rattling on the frying pan. 'Why should I be scared?'

Dalian McGuffie (8)
Woodnewton Junior School, Corby

HOME ALONE

All alone in my room, watching TV, it was a cold dark night in the middle of winter. Mum and Dad were out shopping.

There was a tapping at the window. I looked out of the window, it was only a branch. There was a squeaking noise again, in the living room. It was my dog squeaking his toy.

My mum and dad came back and no more strange things happened.

Kelsey Raffo (8)
Woodnewton Junior School, Corby

ALL ALONE

All alone Linda sat in her bedroom. It was a hot summer's night. Her mum was at work, she had no one to look after her. Her dad had died and her brother and sister were out, she had no one to talk to. She was watching TV. Linda was scared because she heard feet coming closer and closer. Her heart was beating. She froze after the strange noise came closer... and closer. It was something. Linda didn't know what it was.

Linda saw a shadow, what was it? Who was it? Then something touched Linda's shoulder. 'Who is that?'
'It's me,' a voice said.
After, Linda felt cold air on her feet, but it was Linda's sister.
Linda said, 'I am safe now. I am in my house, so we can have a feast and we will watch a scary movie.'

Linda was never scared after that. Linda heard some footsteps. Oh no, not again. But she wasn't scared.

Jennifer Morgan (8)
Woodnewton Junior School, Corby

WALKING HOME

All alone in the dark street, Paul walked, hearing strange noises. It was a freezing Thursday night. Paul was walking home from his friend's house. The strange noises were getting louder. Paul was getting closer. The strange noises were chasing him wherever he went. Closer, closer, louder, louder . . . until the strange noises stopped. The street lights turned off, the house lights turned off. It was pitch-black.

Paul started to run home. He tripped over on the ground. Paul heard footsteps getting closer. He felt something touching him, picking him up.
'Help!' shouted Paul.

Next, all the street lights came on. All the house lights came on. Finally, he was at his front door. Paul was safe with his family.

Ryan Britton (8)
Woodnewton Junior School, Corby

SOMETHING ROUND THE CORNER

A long way away in Africa, there were three boys who were trapped in a rainforest. *Bang!*
'What was that?' Joe asked Jack with a scared voice.
'I think it was a jaguar.'
'Jaguar!' Jack screeched.
Luke heard it creep round the tent. Just then, Joe thought of a plan.
'I know what we can do, we can shout 'blah-di blah-di blah!'' he explained.
'Are you ready?' Jack asked.
'Yes.'
'Blah-di, blah-di, blah!'
The creature crept round the tent. *Scratch!*
'Th-th-the creature.'
It slipped into the tent as quick as a lightning bolt. *Bang!* The creature was shot.
'Dad! Phew!' Joe said in relief.

Luke Slater (7)
Woodnewton Junior School, Corby

STUCK IN A MAZE

One scary night. Thomas woke up at 11.30pm. He thought it was day and went out to play. He found a rusty door. When Thomas opened it, he found himself in a dark maze. He was scared. Thomas sat in a corner, terrified. The bushes rattled, the trees waved in the breeze. Thomas whispered to himself, 'I think I'm lost.'

Thomas tried to crawl through the deep hedge. It was dark. He couldn't fit. He wished he'd never eaten the bag of sweets. Thomas shouted, 'Help!' as loud as he could, but nobody could hear him. Silence. Thomas sat stiffly.

Scared, Thomas tried to find his way out. He came to a dead end. He sat on a rock, worried. Slowly, the rock moved. Thomas didn't know it was moving. The rock moved. Thomas landed on a button. A door opened behind him. He went out of the maze and back home. Thomas was relieved.

Brandon Midlane (7)
Woodnewton Junior School, Corby

IN THE RAINFOREST

Tia was in the rainforest. She was deep into the rainforest. Tia heard crunching of leaves behind her. Everything was still. Tia got so scared. The wind blew hard. She saw a tail of an animal. Tia got so worried. She tried to climb a tree, but she couldn't. Tia ran. As she was running, she looked for somewhere to hide. Tia found tall grass. She quickly hid in it. Tia heard sniffing, ran and found a lake. Tia dived in and held her breath. She got out at the other end. When she got out, she started to run. Tia heard a gunshot and looked behind her, then animal was dead.

Nicola Gemmell (8)
Woodnewton Junior School, Corby

SPOOKS!

A door went *bang.* They jumped with fright. They were scared of the bang. Slowly they walked to the door, but the door slammed shut and locked. They were stuck inside the museum. When Hayley turned around, there was a skeleton. 'Arghhh!' she screamed.
'It is only a model,' Rachel whispered. '
'I think we're not the only ones here.'
Crash, smash, bash!
'What was that?' Calum cried.
Hayley gulped.
'Don't be silly,' yawned Jack.
They all went round the museum.
Calum cried, 'Look, there is a gap in the wall.'
But all it was, was an old broken chair. Scared, Hayley felt fingers up her spine. They all heard footsteps. Jack looked around the corner, but it was their mum. She took them to the kitchen in the museum.

Hayley Gray (8)
Woodnewton Junior School, Corby

BROK AND THE FOX

One day, Brok went in the woods and went deep into them and was trying to hunt a fox. He saw one, but he never got it. He hunted and he hunted and he saw a fox's den. There was a *squeak*. 'Who was that?' said Brok.
It was a fox. He ran for his life. The fox ran after him, he climbed up a tree. The fox went. Brok climbed down and went for a walk and stopped. 'Why did the fox chase me?' he said, then he just kept on walking and walking. He fell asleep.

The next day, he kept on walking and saw that nasty old fox and almost got killed, and he went back to the tent and went to sleep.

On the third day he kept on travelling and travelling, and the fox came back and Brok got his gun and shot him.

Jack Sheridan (8)
Woodnewton Junior School, Corby

THE ABANDONED MUSEUM

One sunny morning, Josi went to call on Joe. They went to the park. Josi ran over the bridge, Joe followed.
He shouted, 'No! That's the abandoned museum.'
'Joe, stop being so scared. Come on.'
So off they went.

Joe opened the door, *creak.* The door slammed shut. They jumped in, 'Uh ho.'
They were trapped, so they looked around for secret doors. But there was no sign of anything.

Suddenly, Josi looked behind her. Something moved. She screeched, then ran to catch up with Joe. They walked on. They walked past many things. They decided to sit down and something came closer and closer.

Suddenly, someone shouted, 'Josi, Joe?' It was Josi's mum.
'Mum, it's you!' shouted Josi.

So that's how it ended. Josi's mum came to get them and they lived happily ever after.

Lauren Honeyman (8)
Woodnewton Junior School, Corby

STUCK IN A HAUNTED MUSEUM

Bang! The museum door slammed. Catherine and Chloe jumped. They didn't know what had just happened.

'Catherine, I'm scared, I want to go now,' whispered Chloe as she shivered.

'Me too, I really do,' shrieked Catherine.

Shake, shake, went the skeletons. The trees were shaking and the leaves were waving round and round. Chloe just wanted to run like dragons' wings flapping.

'Catherine, I want to go now, and I hear shaking,' cried Chloe.

'Let's try and see if the windows are open,' squeaked Catherine.

But as soon as they got closer, they felt a breeze, a bigger, bigger breeze. As they followed the breeze, it got stronger. Catherine found a hole in the wall.

'Can you fit in it?'

Just then, the keeper shouted, 'Help! Please pass my keys.'

'Here you go,' shouted Catherine.

So he opened the door and Chloe and Catherine were saved.

Catherine Creedon (8)
Woodnewton Junior School, Corby

MOUNTAIN EXPERIENCE!

Veer, veer, veer, veer!
'That doesn't sound good,' whispered Jack.
'I agree,' said Mollie.
All of a sudden, Jack and Mollie's torch ran out. Silence. It was pitch-black.
'Help, oh Lord, help!' Mollie cried.
Jack ran over where the bats were.
'Mollie, oh come on, Mollie, we don't have time for games.'
Suddenly, all the bats flew all around him.
'Ah, there you are Mollie,' Jack grabbed a bat and set off.

Meanwhile, Mollie was heading over to a rock. She sat on it. Then a ginormous tarantula crawled up her arm. It was just about to bite her when . . .
'Ah, there you are Jack!'
'Let's get out of here!'
Jack, the bat, Mollie and the spider bumped into each other.
'Jack?'
'Mollie?'
'Wow, wait a minute, if you're there . . . who's this?'
'I don't know,' Jack replied.
Suddenly, Mollie knew exactly what she was holding. It had eight legs, eight eyes and it was furry. 'Argh!' Mollie screamed.
Jack suddenly jumped into thin air. He knew what he was holding. It had two wings, two fangs. 'Argh!' Jack was holding a bat!

They shook off the spider and bat. They both thought of ideas. First they climbed up to see if there was a hole. Then they could climb through it. Jack and Mollie quietly climbed the cave. They looked down. Silence. Cold air shot up Jack's shirt.
'Brrr,' whispered Jack.
'I don't see any light,' shouted Mollie. 'We're doomed!'
Next, they tied a rope around each other. 'Let's split up. You go right and I'll go left.'
'OK,' shouted Mollie.
They both set off.

Bang!
'Argh!' cried Jack.
'There's something chasing me!' Mollie screeched. *'Help me!'*
'OK.' Jack pulled Mollie over to him. 'I don't think we should do that.'
'Yeah,' Molly gasped. 'I know, we'll feel our footprints and they will lead us to the entrance.
'OK.'
So they went. Just then, Mollie found a spider and Jack found a bat.
'Let's not do that.'
'Yeah!
Their bodies stood stiff.

Whilst Mollie and Jack were thinking, a mountain climber was coming.
Tap, tap.
'What was that!' screamed Mollie.
Silence.
'Argh!'
The mountain climber heard this. He tied a rope around him and led them out of the cave. He took the kids home and gave them both a cup of cocoa.

Cerys Russell (8)
Woodnewton Junior School, Corby

GRAVEYARD TROUBLE

Crash! Jess jumped.
'Are you OK, Jess?' said Joe.
'Yes, I am fine.'
'Woo-oooo,' said Jack.
'Thanks for bringing your glasses, Jack,' said Jess.
'Don't mention it,' giggled Jack, getting all proud of himself.
'Oh Jack, snap out of it,' smirked Joe
'Oh, oh . . . s-sorry folks,' muttered Jack.
'OK, I will let you off the hook this time, but any more and you're leaving,' sighed Joe.
'OK,' moaned Jack in a low down voice.

They were just reading a tombstone when they heard a noise. They decided to leave when a tombstone fell down and blocked their path. First, Jess tried kicking the tombstones into their original space. 'Ouch!' said Jess.
'Well now we know for sure that that idea won't work. Are you OK Jess?' said Joe.
'Yes I'm fine, I just hurt my foot.'
'I bet you did. That looked like a hell of a kick.'
'Oww, owww!'
Jack heard Jess crying with agony in the background. When Jess got back up, she fell back into Jack's arms.
'Joe, can you take her for me please,' groaned Jack.
'Fine, fine, fine,' sighed Joe.
'My foot's better now, much better,' gasped Jess.
Jack shouted, 'I have a brilliant idea. We could jam my glasses in the tombstone.'
'Yes, yes, yes. We've done it,' they all shouted.
Just then, Jack's mum came up to see what all the fuss was about.
'Boys, what's all the fuss about? Oh, sorry, boys and girls, what's all the fuss about?'
'Well we've got lots to tell you. The tombstones were moving and all sorts of weird things were happening.' They panicked.

'You silly billys, it was just the alley cats. Didn't you know the tombstones were all loose? Well, you come home and tell me all about the adventure.'

From then onwards, they never went to the graveyard at night again.

Jessica Bellew (8)
Woodnewton Junior School, Corby

HANDS AT NIGHT

One sunny day, Lauren and her best friend, Nicola, went to the arcade. They met their mate Luke. Lauren and Nicola went on nearly every game in the arcade. When they finished, it was dark. Lauren had to go through the graveyard to get home. So they all set off to go home. Lauren walked through the graveyard. A hand suddenly pulled on Lauren's leg. 'Help, please somebody help!' Lauren squealed.

She tried to climb out of the hand, but she couldn't. Then Nicola came to the rescue. She poured water over the hand.
A voice shouted, 'What did you do that for?'
It sounded like Luke.
Lauren pulled the hand up. She saw Luke. Lauren shouted in Luke's ear, 'Go away!' Then Lauren ran away with Nicola. They were never friends again.

Kaisie Flanagan (7)
Woodnewton Junior School, Corby

Lost In The Woods

The leaves rustled in the howling wind. Michael and Graham walked slowly through the thick leaves on the forest floor. 'In a minute, we need to stop and look for a spot to set the tent up,' Michael said.

By dusk, Michael and Graham had set up camp. The high trees were creaking and groaning in the chilly wind. A grey mist floated slowly in through the trees. 'I'm freezing, Michael, I'm going to get firewood,' Graham moaned.

When Graham had gone to collect firewood, Michael started to unpack the rucksacks. Suddenly a branch fell. Michael froze. What was that? It couldn't be Graham because he was out collecting firewood. Michael's heart pounded like dragons' hooves. *Thud, thud.*

Cautiously, Michael started to walk through the dark trees. His big feet crushed the dead leaves. What was that? A shadow slid silently through the branches. Was it a rabbit? No, all the rabbits were asleep. Michael felt his tummy lurch, like a ship rolling in the rough sea.

Michael trod heavily over jagged, grey boulders. In front of him, he could see an old wooden hut, the broken window banging in the wind. Michael wondered if anybody lived there. Carefully, Michael stepped on the creaking floorboards. His shaking hands pushed the door open. '*Boo!* Did I scare you?'

Rebecka Heath (8)
Woodnewton Junior School, Corby

LOST IN THE FOREST

The leaves rustled in the howling wind. Michael and Graham walked slowly through the thick forest. 'Not long now till we put up the tent,' said Graham.

By dusk, Michael and Graham had set up camp. The tall trees were creaking in the howling wind. A chilly gust of wind knocked the tent over.
'I'm freezing!' moaned Graham. 'I'm going to get some firewood. You stay here and fix the tent.'

When Graham had gone to collect the firewood, Michael started to fix the tent. A twig snapped. Michael froze. What was that? It couldn't be Graham because he had just gone to get some firewood. Michael's heart was racing fast as a racing car.

Carefully, Michael started to walk through the shadowy trees. His healthy feet crunching the dead leaves. What was that? A shadow shot as quick as a gun, in the branches. Was that a bat? No, it was not the right time for bats. Michael felt a frozen shiver run down his neck. Carefully, very carefully, Michael looked around the brown trunk of the tree. His pale face looked like he was sick.
'Boo! Got ya!' laughed Graham.

Demi Weston (8)
Woodnewton Junior School, Corby

LOST IN THE WOODS

The rain splashed in the muddy puddles. Michael and Graham walked slowly through the soggy leaves. 'We might need to stop and put up the tent soon,' suggest Graham.

By dusk, Michael and Graham had set up camp. The tall trees were creaking and groaning in the howling wind. It was getting foggy and there were lots of shadows around. It was chilly now. 'I'm freezing,' moaned Graham. 'I'm going to get some firewood. You stay and guard our stuff.'

When Graham had gone to collect firewood, Michael started to unpack the rucksacks. Suddenly, a branch fell. Michael froze. What was that? It couldn't be a person because nobody was around. Michael's heart pounded like somebody stamping their feet in an empty room.
Bang, bang, bang.

Cautiously, Michael started to walk through the shadowy trees, his sore feet crunching the dead leaves. What was that? A shadow slid silently through the branches. Was it a squirrel? No, it was the wrong time of the day for squirrels. Michael's sweating hands shook. Michael looked round the edge of a tree.
'Boo! Did I scare you?' laughed Graham.

Melissa Ward (8)
Woodnewton Junior School, Corby

LOCKED IN THE LIBRARY

Jake and Ricky got lost in the library. Just when they were going to go home, the door locked. *Slam!* Jake looked at Ricky, 'The door is locked,' he said.
'There must be another way out,' suggested Ricky.

It had been an hour and Jake and Ricky were starving.
Jake shouted, 'Let me out!'
Ricky had an idea. Jake would get a pile of books and make some stairs. Jake went to get to get some books. Ricky heard a noise and saw a shadow. What was that? Ricky froze. A lot of books fell. Ricky jumped. 'What was that?' he said.
It was just Jake and their mums and dads.

Ricky Murray (8)
Woodnewton Junior School, Corby

CAMPING IN THE WOODS

The tent fell and ripped in the wind. Alice and Demi looked sadly at the huge hole in the tent.
'We have to mend it,' said Demi.

By dusk, Demi and Alice had mended the tent. It was getting gloomy and chilly. There were a lot of shadows.
'I think I'll go and get firewood. It's freezing,' yelled Demi.

When Demi had gone, Alice started to set everything up. Suddenly, a twig snapped. What was that? It couldn't be thunder and lightning because that stopped two hours ago. Alice was shaking all over, like a bag of ice cubes.

Cautiously, Alice strolled through the dull trees, her feet standing on the broken twigs. What was that? A shadow slipped as quick as a racing car. What was that? Was it a bat? No, bats are not in the woods. Alice froze down her spine.
Then Demi came back . . . *'Boo!'*
'Aargh!'
'I knew you would be scared,' laughed Demi.

Deanna Barley (7)
Woodnewton Junior School, Corby

ALONE IN THE WOODS

The leaves of the trees blew in the strong wind. Graham and Michael carried on ahead, through the dark woods, to see where they could put their tent up. 'Let's put the tent up now,' said Graham.

By dusk, Michael and Graham had set their tent up. The trees were creaking and groaning in the howling wind. The wind was so strong it blew the tent over. 'I'm freezing,' said Graham. 'I'm going to get firewood. You stay here and carry on putting the tent up.'

When Graham had gone, Michael kept on putting the tent up. Suddenly, he heard a stick fall. Michael turned slowly. What was that? It couldn't be Graham, because he'd just left. Michael's arms and legs shivered. Michael walked through the dark trees. His feet were hurting him. Dead leaves rustled. What was it? Was it a bat? No, they don't come out at this time. Michael felt a cold sweat coming down his spine. Carefully, he peered round the dark tree.
'Boo!' laughed Graham.

Kate Inglis (8)
Woodnewton Junior School, Corby

Alone In The Woods

The howling wind forced Michael and Graham back. When the wind calmed down, they set up their tent in a bundle of flowers.
'We will need to go and collect firewood,' said Graham.
The trees were getting breezy again.

After a while, when they had set up their tent, the trees were rustling through the chilly wind. The tree leaves moved wildly from side to side. 'I'm freezing,' shouted Graham. 'I'll go and get some firewood. You stay here and guard the camp.'

When Graham had gone to collect firewood, Michael had brought some potatoes, he was peeling them for tea. A branch snapped. Michael turned. What was that? A shadow fell as quick as a ghost. Was it a squirrel? No, it was too hot for squirrels. He felt a shiver down his spine.
'Boo! Gotcha!' laughed Graham.

Demi Garvey (8)
Woodnewton Junior School, Corby

IN THE WOODS

The daisies danced in the red-hot sun. Michael and Graham were staring at the huge hole in their tent.
'We'd better fix it up then,' said Graham.

By dusk, Michael and Graham had fixed the tent. The howling wind was blowing the wild leaves nearer and nearer to the gloomy campsite. Michael jumped and slipped in the dark, black, chilly mist.
'I'm freezing,' moaned Graham. 'You stay here and guard the tent.'

When Graham had gone, Michael started to unpack the bags. Suddenly, a branch cracked. Michael froze! What was that? It couldn't be the wind, because that had now settled. Michael's heart pounded like a banging door. *Bang, bang, bang!*

Cautiously, Michael started to walk through the shadowy trees. *I think I will go and help Graham get firewood,* Michael thought. When he got out of the tent, he pulled his heavy feet along in the forest. What was that? A shadow shot as quick as a knife through the wavy trees. Was it a fox? It couldn't be a fox because they only come out at night. Michael felt a chilly shiver run down his spine.

Demi Johnson (7)
Woodnewton Junior School, Corby

ALONE IN THE WOODS

The heavy raindrops splashed in the deep puddles. Michael and Graham jumped excitedly in the muddy puddles, while watching the daffodils dancing.

'We can stop and put the tent up here,' suggested Graham.

By dusk, Michael and Graham had set up camp. The trees were rustling and the moon shone brightly through the chilly trees. The snails slimed through the dark fog. 'It's freezing,' groaned Graham. 'I'll go and fetch firewood, but you stay here and guard the tent.'

When Graham had gone to collect firewood, Michael started to unpack the rucksacks. A branch fell. Michael froze. What was that? It couldn't be Graham because he just left camp five minutes ago to collect firewood. Michael's heart was pounding loudly, like a hammer banging on a wall. *Bang, bang, bang.*

Cautiously, Michael walked steadily through the crunching leaves. Michael stopped! What was that? A shadow glided as smooth as a ghost. Was that a squirrel? No, it's too late to be a squirrel. His thighs shivered coldly.

'Ha! Gotcha!' laughed Graham.

Courtney Crawford (8)
Woodnewton Junior School, Corby

Lost In The Woods

Michael screwed his eyes up in the burning sun in the middle of the warm woods. Graham's mouth was really dry because he needed something to drink.
'We have to find a clear space to put up our tent,' said Michael.

By dusk, Michael and Graham had set up camp. The shadows of the trees were getting bigger. The sky was getting black. The flaps of the tent were flapping in the whistling wind.
'I'm freezing,' moaned Graham. 'I'm going to get some firewood. You stay here and guard our stuff.'

When Graham had gone to collect some firewood, Michael started to open their sleeping bags. Suddenly, the leaves rustled. Michael gasped! 'What was that noise?' It couldn't be Graham because he was collecting firewood. Michael's heart pounded loudly, like loud footsteps on a patio coming nearer and nearer. *Bang, bang!*

Cautiously, Michael strolled through the damp trees, his shivery feet walking on the pointy sticks. What was that? A shadow shot as quick as a racing car through the crackly leaves. What was that? Was it a bat? No, it was the wrong time of year for black bats. Michael started to feel frozen. Sweat was running down his back.
'Boo!' laughed Graham. 'What? Can't you take a joke?'

Emily Tierney (8)
Woodnewton Junior School, Corby

SCARED IN THE WOODS

The wind echoed through the woods and the flowers stood up proudly in the shining sun. Michael and Graham were watching the holly daisies blowing in the gentle breeze.

'Can we put the tent up now and make a fire?' asked Graham.

When Graham had gone to collect the firewood, Michael was unpacking their rucksacks. Suddenly, a branch fell. Michael gulped. 'What was that strange noise?' It couldn't be lightning, because it was sunny. Michael's hands started to sweat and his heart was thumping loudly, like the beat of human footsteps. *Thump, bang, thump, bang, thump, thud, bang!*

Michael crept slowly through the dark, cold woods to explore what was making that sound.

Suddenly, a shadow shot quick as a bullet. What was that? Was it a bat? No, there are no bats in this country. It was coming closer and closer, and then Michael got fed up and he followed the mysterious figure into a graveyard. Then Michael peered round a grave and looked fooled. 'You scaredy cat!' said Graham.

Kimberley Briglin (8)
Woodnewton Junior School, Corby

ON YOUR OWN IN THE WOODS

Michael watched the flowers standing up straight in the rain. The raindrops were splashing into muddy puddles.
'Let's set up camp and make a fire,' said Graham.

By dusk, Michael and Graham had set up camp. The trees were swinging side to side in the wind and it had become chilly. The wind nearly blew the tent down and Michael said, 'I'm freezing. Go and get some firewood.'

When Graham had gone to get firewood, Michael started to fill up the pot with water. Suddenly, an apple fell. What did that? It couldn't be thunder because that had stopped. Michael was sweating. He got out of the tent and glanced round the trunk of a tree. Michael's heart was racing like thunder.
'Boo! Scared you, scaredy cat!' laughed Graham.

Ciara Haughey (8)
Woodnewton Junior School, Corby

LOST IN THE WOODS

Michael and Graham were walking down into the woods. Graham and Michael saw lots of grey squirrels jumping up the trees. 'We need to build the tent now,' said Michael.

By dusk, Michael and Graham had just set up camp. It was chilly and the wind was blowing the tent flaps. 'It's late, very late, shall I go and get the firewood?'
'Go on then,' said Graham.

Graham had just unpacked the sleeping bags and put them on the bunk bed. Graham started to get the potatoes and peeled them. Graham was getting scared and worried. He heard a noise, it couldn't have been Michael because he had only just gone. Graham heard it again. It was like a dragon's foot, *bang, bang, bang.* Graham went to look for him. He saw something. He went to a tree.
'Boo!' said Michael. 'Got you there!'

Jake Martin (8)
Woodnewton Junior School, Corby

A Ghost Story

I was happy when I was walking home, because it was my very first time. I was quite nervous as well, but that didn't change a thing, so I kept walking.

The road was dark and seemed to go on forever. The lamps were on and were shining so brightly that they made shadowy monsters from the trees. Everything was so still, it froze. Just then, a light from a lamp post went off. I wondered why this was happening. Then a bunch of leaves fell from a tree. I could hear soft footsteps behind me, slowly they started to run. I was trembling now. I tripped over a stone and it dug into my skin. My back was stinging hard. I had sweat coming from my head. Dark clouds came swiftly over and it started to rain. I turned around.

Suddenly, a shadow flitted behind me. I was soaking now. Nothing moved. My heart was beating so fast, I couldn't feel it. I felt dizzy and confused, my head was going through things that might happen. I was hungry. I wished I could go home.

Suddenly, something grabbed both of my shoulders, I screamed as loud as I could. Then something strangled me round my neck. I thought I was going to die. I knew this was going to be the end of me.
'Why are you screaming? I just wanted a piggy-back home,' said my little brother.
'Because you were strangling me and I've got a pain in my back,' I lied.

Eventually I got home, but I couldn't sleep. Do you think it really was a ghost?

Sarah Russell (8)
Woodnewton Junior School, Corby

A Ghost Story

It was twilight. I was all alone on a dark road. The trees looked like monsters. The sky looked like ink. It was dull. All was silent, all was still. Nothing moved. I felt nobody else was in the world with me, or nobody loved me. I didn't like being alone, especially on the road.

All of a sudden, a shadow flitted between the trees. I heard soft, padding footsteps behind me. Then I thought I heard a tiny rustle. I heard a scraping at the ground. What was it? Was it animal? Was it human? I was frightened. What could be happening to me? What was behind me? Was anybody trying to catch me? I didn't know. Then I was really scared. I heard some soft footsteps now, coming faster and faster. Someone's hot breath was sinking into my shoulder. I fell to the ground. Something was coming up my face (it was soft).

I hid my face, counted to ten, then got up. My brother was standing there with my dog, Pepper. I said, 'Were you running?'
My brother said, 'No!'
I thought to myself, *he must have been running.* I thought and thought and thought again. Then I said to myself, 'There must be someone else on this road and my brother got here just in time.'

Jessica Coull (8)
Woodnewton Junior School, Corby

A Ghost Story

I was on my way home from school when I suddenly noticed I hadn't got my book bag, so I went back to the school. When I went to get my book bag, it wasn't on my peg. Then I remembered, I had put it in my drawer, so I went back into the classroom and looked in my drawer, but it wasn't there. Something strange was going on.

Suddenly, I heard some keys go into the keyhole. Someone was coming, because I could hear their soft, padding footsteps coming close and closer and closer to the classroom. I looked around the corner, but no one was there. I looked the other way, but no one was on that side either. When I looked around the corners, the footsteps stopped, so I went back into the classroom and started to look for my book bag again.

Suddenly, I heard the footsteps again. I got more and more scared. My heart was beating like a drum. Then I saw the classroom door handle turn. I said to myself, 'I am dead meat.' What was it? Who was it? Was it a ghost haunting me? The handle turned slower and slower, I was shaking and shivering. I stood further and further back, then I hid under the table. The door swung open, then I saw my brother's shoes and then I got up. I said to my brother, 'How did you get in?'
'Your teacher gave me her keys.'
I said, 'Oooh ooh.'
Then he said, 'Oh, and by the way, you left your book bag at home, so I brought it for you.'
Then I said, 'Can we just go home now?'

Charlotte Roberts (8)
Woodnewton Junior School, Corby

A Ghost Story

In the dark, dark wood I was alone, well, I thought I was. I stood there listening. I saw an owl. It looked at me, I looked back at it. It hooted as loud as it could, *hoot!*

I carried on walking. Suddenly, I heard a faint rustle in the bush right beside me. I turned round to look, a shadow ran into a tree. I froze like I was a statue. I thought it was the end. My eyes were fading. I just saw the shape of the trees. I suddenly thought I could move, first my arms, then my legs. I woke up, I stood up. I was a bit dizzy first, but then I started to wake up. I could see someone or something right in front of me. It looked like my reflection. I blinked and looked again. It was my sister. 'Why are you here?' I said.
'I came to look for you.'
'Why?'
'Because Mum is worried. Come on, we'd better go home now.'

We kept walking. By now we could see the house. I went in and straight to bed. I couldn't get to sleep for ages.

In the morning:

'Come on, there's a big day ahead of us.'
'Where are we going then?'
'Not to tell.'

Nicola Miller (7)
Woodnewton Junior School, Corby